DRACULA
BEYOND STOKER

Issue 1

DBS Press

Dracula Beyond Stoker
Issue 1

Tucker Christine
editor

Edward G. Pettit
consulting editor

Published by DBS Press
ISBN - 979-8-9867340-0-2 (Paperback)
ISBN - 979-8-9867340-1-9 (e-book)
November, 2022

www.dbspress.com
www.draculabeyondstoker.com

All works copyright ©2022 their respective authors
Except *Father Pace* ©2012 Samuel Marzioli
Reprinted with author's permission
Cover by Jeff Wong
All Rights Reserved

Contents

29 October

My Friends,

Welcome to the debut issue of Dracula Beyond Stoker, a celebration of Bram Stoker's novel, and a continuation of its legacy.

I trust that since you're here you share my love of all things Dracula.

I have been in thrall to Stoker's novel from a very young age and have learned through multiple readings and conversations that — like the vampire — this story is ever changing. From reader to reader and even reading to reading it can shift from gothic romance to thrilling adventure to gripping mystery to sensational horror. Most of the characters are somehow simultaneously richly drawn and blank-slate archetypes that readers can imprint upon and make their own. Stoker drew on and distilled existing folklore, which continues to morph as time goes on, these modern additions to the lore color the way we view the text whether we want it to or not. These are some of the qualities that leave Dracula open to so many interpretations and allow the story to live on.

This issue presents ten visions of Dracula, himself, in a variety of styles, settings, and formats.

Chris McAuley — one of the architects of the StokerVerse with Bram's great-grandnephew, Dacre Stoker — appropriately gets us started with a gruesome origin story dictated by a cruel Count, while H. Parsons presents a slightly more empathetic side culled from Dracula's own journal.

Daniel Dorsch's *The Tale of the Szgany* gives us a glimpse of Dracula's relationship with the gypsies living outside of his castle.

Henry Herz offers a modern-day mystery with many pop-culture nods starring Dracula in the role of supernatural detective.

Elizabeth — a one-act play by Gerard J. Waggett — imagines a tense meeting with Elizabeth Bathory in a very unpleasant location.

Jessica Gleason's *The Night Museum* is contemporary (in both style and setting), humorous, and romantic; Jill Protokowicz's Count is sentimental.

John Kiste will have you laughing out loud. And I don't really know how to describe *The Historical Dracula*. Sam Ruddick's piece is surreal and clever and unsettling.

Lastly, Samuel Marzioli, in an updated version of a tale he wrote for *Stupefying Stories* (issue 1.8, October 2012), reveals Dracula's final confession to *Father Pace*.

We also have an appreciation and examination of Blacula, arguably the most often overlooked and under appreciated of Dracula's countless avatars, from Toothpickings, and we finish it all up with a poetic treatise on film, adaptation, and immortality from Jessica Lévai.

This is the first step in what I anticipate to be a long and happy journey. I'm glad you're here for it.

Your Friend,

Tucker

FRESH BLOOD

Dracula: Origins
Celebrating 125 Years of Dracula
By Chris McAuley

Aidan watched, his eyes growing large with fear, as his brother monk was pressed to the cold stone floor. Soldiers in tattered robes pressed their weight against his arms and back. A voice rich with power resounded across the hall.

"Spread his legs. We must teach this dishonest priest the cost of lying to Vlad Dracul."

Aidan tore his attention away from Father Alphege's plight. He gazed at the figure on the throne. Dracula was a broad-shouldered titan, his face was like chiseled marble. His scarlet clothing trimmed with the finest fur. It had been claimed that he had dipped his tunic and robes in the blood of the Turks. It was also claimed that he drank babies' blood and performed Satanic rituals. With the cruelty which Aidan had witnessed, he could believe these rumors to be true.

Dracula noticed the shift in the monk's attention. Clasping his hands together he nodded to the drama unfolding in his hall.

"Direct yourself to your brother monk's situation. As your God instructs, so do I."

Aidan noticed that Father Alphege's legs were now spread and his simple grey habit pulled upwards. His exposed body showed the emaciation which was the result of weeks of malnourishment. The two monks had made the decision to visit the Voivode's castle out of desperation. Dracula had taken the farmers and flax workers into his army. They never returned. Reports came back that they had all been killed in military action against the Sultan. Rumors also persisted that Dracula had sacrificed them, leaving their grotesque remains as a warning to the Turkish army.

If I could do this to my own people, what would I do to you?

The Great Hall's doors opened and three soldiers carried in a wooden block. Aidan could see that the tip had been hewed and sharpened into a point. Shuddering, he once again recalled the stories concerning the missing villagers.

Father Alphege saw the stake coming towards him with his left eye. His face was pressed squarely against the stone floor by the heel of a soldier's boot. He struggled against his attackers in vain. Their weight meant that he could do little more than shift his body slightly. Father Alphege felt hands grip his skeletal legs and force them open. A voice came from behind him, giving instructions to the men at arms holding him.

"Grease him up!"

Alphege felt a hot sticky substance cover his rear, he recognized the smell instantly. They were coating him with pigs' fat. The soldier holding his left arm leaned into his ear.

"Sometimes virgins need a little help, Father."

The stake was inserted. Its stout frame forced up into the monk's rectum and into his colon. The soldiers laughed at Father Alphege's moans and squeals. The sharp end of the wood tore through his insides and ruptured his intestines. Fluids of various colors leaked from Alphege's rectal cavity and streamed down the wood pole.

Dracula rose from his throne and motioned for his soldiers to take the impaled man outside.

"Take our duplicitous priest out into the courtyard. Hammer him into the ground. Place a sign above him to state his crime. I do not want my people to think I executed him unjustly."

Aidan fell to his knees at the horror he had witnessed. Tears streamed from his eyes. Alphege had been particularly kind to Aidan when he was brought to the monastery. Like many novices, Aidan had been lost and alone when entering through the iron gates. His parents had no more room for him and had barely enough to feed themselves. Once he accepted the responsibilities of the novitiate, his brother monks had become his family.

Dracula watched the young monk and observed his expression of terror melt into righteous fury. Stroking his moustache thoughtfully, he addressed Aidan. His sonorous baritone penetrating through the haze of anger which permeated the monk's thoughts.

"Perhaps you will be more honest when I ask the same question I posed to your friend. Do you think that I will reach heaven when I die?"

Watching Dracula take his throne once again, the monk stood. His hands clenched into fists as he spoke. His voice was as strong and true as any of the nobles who had entered the Voivode's court.

"My Lord, it is true that I am fearful of you. I watched my mentor and brother die at your hands and I know what fate could await me as I speak. I was also taught that the beginning of wisdom is the fear of God and that his judgement is eternal, so now I speak what I truly know. For your vile acts and cruel judgements against your fellow man, you will surely descend to Hell. God himself will tear you from your throne and strip you of all your titles. Naked, you will be thrown to the pit and reside with the devil himself. There will be no mercy for you."

Dracula watched as Aidan gave his answer. The monk's hands were clenched so hard that drops of blood ran from his fists. The scarlet fluid dripped onto the simple grey tunic and onto the black stone floor.

Nodding slowly, Dracula once again motioned for his soldiers to come forward. Aidan felt dizzy but resolute. As the soldiers grabbed his arms he was prepared for his impending and grizzly death.

A table was set in front of Dracula, parchment and ink were brought, and, as Aidan was forced into the wooden chair, a quill pen was shoved into his hand.

"Many of the Turks believe that my life is a blasphemy against the face of their God. I tell you, priest, that my life began before your Christ existed."

As Dracula continued, he pointed to the painting of the crucifixion. It showed the Roman soldier piercing the side of Christ.

"It was I who killed your God. I pierced his heart with my spear. His sweet, sacred blood ran down my face and was captured by my tongue. In that moment, the Sun hid its face from me. I was, for one of the very few moments in my life, in ecstasy."

Aidan stared at the Count, was he really inferring that he was Longinus? Had Vlad III, protectorate of Romania finally lost his mind?

Dracula gazed at the monk, his eyes narrowed and his voice became like flint.

"You will write of my past, so that I may not lose it in the future. Others of my kind have warned me that with long life comes the possibility of forgetfulness. After you have recorded the story I tell, you have my word that I shall let you go."

As Dracula began to speak, the monk wrote, and an account of the first vampire began.

"Before recorded history, I was a rage-filled soul. I would observe the hunters stake their claims on the grasslands. If successful they would bring their kills back to their families. The caves would dance with the heat and light of the fire and the tribes' bellies would be full. I was not a hunter; I was a thief and a murderer. I would lie in wait for the tribesmen to return home, pulling the carcass of their prey on their sleds. Eventually, driven by hunger and hatred I would leap from my ledge and beat them to death.

"I am now ashamed of this existence; it is why I treat theft and murder so harshly in our lands. You must remember, monk, that this was before written laws, an era where moral code was dictated by the elders and shamans of the tribe.

"It was a winter day that my sins finally caught up with me. I had followed a hunter out to the killing grounds and watched him trap his prey with ease. He was evidently skilled and potentially dangerous. I was ravenous, however, and the sight of the deer which he had captured made my insides growl. He took out a knife and prepared the carcass, remembering to thank the animal for its sacrifice as he did so.

"As he returned home, I stalked him as carefully as he had the deer. As he reached the first set of caves, he must have sensed me. I congratulated myself that I had been able to stay hidden for so long. In this way, I had been from birth, a natural hunter of men. As he turned, I smashed my fists into his face, breaking his nose and jaw. He was strong and, like a lion sensing its end, fought hard against my assault. I was determined, however, and soon had him on the ground. It was then that I raised a nearby rock over my head and smashed it into his face. In that moment his skull fractured and his face both expanded and sagged at the same time. I was exhilarated with the kill and filled with pride. I had taken down a highly skilled foe with my bare hands.

"I watched in wonder as his chest heaved and blood vomited from his lips. I brought my face close to his and drank it all in. This was the first time that I had not ran away after killing a man. I had never felt the spirit leave another human being. As he breathed his last, I whooped in joy and glee. I had caused this. I had taken this life, a man who would never breathe again.

"It was then that I sunk my teeth into human flesh for the first time. Amid the cold winter darkness, I chewed and swallowed the forbidden meat. I dug my nails into his chest and scooped out whatever I could find as my mouth sank into his cheeks. I gorged myself on his blood and I felt happy and sated.

"In my ecstasy, I did not notice that the man's family and other members of the tribe were watching me. As the men cautiously approached me with their clubs in hand, I took my leave. I scrambled onto the nearby ledges and ran towards the secluded forest where I lived. I could not suppress my glee and excitement as I did so. I am sure that my howls of delight carried across the winds to the tribe as the night deepened.

"It was the custom of the time for the dead to be wrapped in cloth and left in a sacred grove with trinkets marking their earthly life. This simple form of spirituality still exists through your church, but you have lost the important symbolism. Coating the body in red ochre and placing the bodies facing the east, towards the Sun.

"I had contempt for this practice and for the priests of the time. The Shamans would take a portion of the meat and clothing from the tribe. They promise a life eternal without proof. In this way they were worse than even I was. Emboldened that night by my kill, I determined that I should go to the sacred grove and desecrate it.

"Unbeknown to me, the Shaman and several men lay in wait. They had guessed that I would attempt to defile the grave site. I was captured as I urinated on the sacred totems and then held down. The holy man sought to cure me by smashing a wooden peg into my skull. It is known today as trepanning and was the process to seek to remove the demons in my brain.

"It is curious how these ancient techniques still find a home now in what we call medicine. The operation was not a success and I lay on the floor of the grove dead with my brains leaking out of my skull.

"My body was slung into the pit reserved for those who had transgressed. It was not blessed by the holy magic of the Shaman. There I would be condemned to lie, my spirit restless and unable to enter into the heavens to be reborn once again.

"I am unsure of the process, but I have memories of encountering demonic gods who whispered me back to life. As I awoke in my body, I felt the numbness of the cold night and heard the padding of footsteps. It had snowed and as I crawled upwards, I felt the soft specks of white touch my face and hair. I still felt pain from the hole in my head, but even worse than this was the gnawing hunger which greeted my resurrection. I was confused for I had been sure that I was dead. I still did not know what I was. Indeed, the name for my kind was not yet invented.

"Wolves encircled the opening of the pit. Their luminous eyes and salivating mouths greeted me as I emerged. Without a moment's thought I pounced on the largest of the group. My canine teeth had grown unnaturally large during my slumber and I used them to rip and tear at my adversary's throat. The others in the pack shied away as their leader succumbed to my attack.

"In moments I had drained the animal of its blood.

"As morning came, I had already moved away from the tribe, from the grave they had left for me. With my brother wolves beside me, I sought answers. This began my travel through the world and the ages."

Dracula was true to his word. When Aidan had penned his story, he was free to return to the monastery. There was a slight caveat to this, however. The Count had contemplated the important aspect of secrecy concerning his true existence. He didn't want superstitious villagers or zealous priests storming his stronghold. So, he ordered Aidan's tongue torn from its root and his hands removed and the stumps cauterized.

A writer who specializes in the Horror, Science Fiction, Fantasy and Crime genres, **Chris McAuley** has been the lead writer in novels, comics, audio dramas and games. He is the co-creator of the popular StokerVerse, along with Bram Stoker's great-grandnephew Dacre Stoker. He has also created a science fiction and fantasy franchise with Babylon 5's Claudia Christian. Chris has worked with some of the top names in Star Wars, Star Trek and Doctor Who. He has recently become the lead writer for a new franchise for Amazon Games.

Friendship and Hospitality
By H. Parsons

CHAPTER XXVIII

Memorandum

After I recovered these articles from the Castle Dracula, I consulted good Doctor Stoyan to whom made it readable to myself and my companions in a swift way. With the help of her translations and Miss Mina's knowledge of her husband's diaries, we attempted to date where there was none and apply chronology where it was otherwise obscure. It worries me to reveal our findings, however. My friend John has been in a way since his recovery and marriage, and I am feared he will be for the rest of his life. Reading the voice of Dracula himself might be too much for his heart — strong and young, yes, but too beaten — to bear.

Much of it was missing; much of it I left behind.

Abraham Van Helsing, M. D., D. Ph., D. Lit., etc., etc.

Fragments of The Journal of Count Dracula, *translated.,*

May. — There was a time in my distant youth when I looked upon this land and felt the fire of life burning in her veins and, in turn, in my own. Red spilt into the soil and nourished her crops; the ferocity of war had strengthened her. But we are in a time of dishonorable peace, of steadfast cowardice to which we have kneeled like lambs to the silent slaughter. I look upon my fair Bistritz and my Carpathians and my nostrils are filled with the bitterness of old blood. Familiar and *fearful* blood. Her people regard me with the terror of deity and come not to my doors except to bring offerings and stain my ears with their pleading. They hang in their homes talismans, and in their hearts prayers that I may not creep through their streets. Their ancestors fought, they cower. They are of their waning generations, I am the last of one.

But O', I am becoming *poetic*.

I grow tired in my isolation and hungry in my solidarity. When I run these aging fingers over my face, I feel the lines of history and fate written into my skin — I have decided if I do not rewrite them, I will fade into their meaning until there is nothing left but a husk.

Humiliating, is it not? For my line to succumb clawing against peace?

I have consulted with a man from London to procure an estate on foreign soil. If my Bistritz has become apprehensive in tradition and thin with caution, their London has lain in modernity and grown fat with contentment. It has been long since I was last regarded a stranger; and where better to hunt than pastures where the prey do not recognize the hunter?

A new blood has entered the valley; it will not be long until I must greet him.

Later. — Many have attempted to warn my guest, I am sure — but to what extent he has understood them I have no certainty. As I rode through their talisman littered roads, the people shirked from me, hiding their faces from my gaze and their bodies from my touch. Bah! I do not want their angst. I found it in my mind, and in what is little left of my *heart*, to not take their feeble attempts as insult. But as I approached, I heard with no ambiguity how the calèche which carried my guest attempted to move him further into Bukovina without my knowledge. The endeavor was quickly abandoned, however, after they saw my face.

I wonder if they would have thought to help him at all if they knew the role he played in their salvation from me?

Surely, they might have. The dying are strange in that respect.

May, cont. — Now that I have met him, I still do not know what I had expected inviting the Englishman into my land. There is an unwitting hubris to them, sending such a fresh blood into this transaction. I had assumed I would be meeting this Hawkins Peter of Exeter, a man who has written with the pen of considerable age and knowledge. But instead, I have been greeted by a Harker Jonathan. He is a funny sort of man. As I gathered him from the calèche, disguised as I was but all too easily recognized, he saw the fear in the people and thought nothing, or at least very little, of it. He said nothing as well, but instead let his gaze fall timidly upon me, and in his eyes I only saw the sheen of blue and a bright wideness of uncertainty of which he looked for answers. He is of fair height, though much smaller than I — a waif build — and topped with a shock of greying black hair I would not have expected on someone so young. He speaks with the age of experience rather than years; this has made me curious to know if all Englishmen carry themselves in such a way, or if I simply have the pleasure of this one. Ay, but I suppose I assumed some different respect of people from a land ruled by monarchy. Maybe he is considered by his superior more than capable of taking on the peculiarities of a boyar, or a *"Count"* as they have taken to calling me. Maybe it is the land that is coming to my possession that gives me an English title. Maybe it is simply what they have decided I am. On assuming I was a servant of this *Count* he has been sent for, I feel he trusted me wholeheartedly, even in the strangeness of what to him is a foreign land.

As we rode through the mists to my castle, my children, the lolling wolves and bats of the night, leapt wildly at our heels. For once, I can sympathize with their enthusiasm; I only wish they would strengthen their resolve. Once I have taken the deeds to the land he offers, their time to sup will come sooner than they know. He is the sample of a greater dish.

What a lamb, this Harker. My women, I feel, will enjoy his youth. I shall too, for the short time of which I will have him.

May, cont., cont.— As I have come to acquaint myself the Englishman has made his own fears known to me. I take his hand and he shudders, in a quiet, reserved manner which I have not seen in my own people. And as I speak to him in his mother's tongue he nods along — unwilling to admit his confusion at the staggering of my words. Is he afraid of this old man who stands above him? I wonder if he would feel differently if this wrinkled face were closer to his own in youth and gaiety.

These papers — this *Carfax,* among my other estates — have already been presented to me. I had planned after the procurement for my use of him to come to an end. He would sup, and in time, so would my children. But in the short span in which we have spoken it seems my friends — even in their ancient vastness — have not taught me all I should know of his fair London.

There is still too much time ahead for impulse or fervor; so why not take carefulness in these matters of delicacy? I will keep the man longer; if his employer is correct about his faithfulness, and if I am correct in his manner, I am sure he will not mind. Or if he does, he will not protest.

Midnight, the same day. — I feel foolish — prideful and foolish in a way I have not felt since I was young. I found dear Jonathan in the library again, reading through the books I have laid out for him and even the ones I had once thought hidden. In my resolve, I set to speak with him on the matters of London and her people. *I would learn,* I decided. *And then I would make quick work of this Englishman.* But instead, he, with an incessant curiosity I had not expected from such a timid creature, poured over my knowledge of this land — of Transylvania — of *myself.* As we spoke the words flew from my lips like breathing, at least from a time in which I required breath, and I told him everything of which he asked, and in turn asked almost nothing of my own.

Somehow hours passed without my awareness, and it was only the tiredness of his face and tested slowing of his heart as the night drew into morning that bid me to quiet myself. *Foolish!* Who is this old man rambling about the *Magyar*, the *Lombard*, the *Avar*, the *Bulgar*, and all those other dead men like a child would their imaginative stories, riddled through their skulls like worms? These are not the times for me to lose track of myself — the nights are short, and there is much to be done. I cannot be distracted telling lived history to one I will, in short time, be seeing dead.

(At least I have learned of this soliciting business. It is dreadful work. I do not understand his passion, but I am glad to hear it.)

The following night. — He writes! Of course, the Englishman writes — and fervently, too. I had hoped to pass his death off as accidental, supposing it was to come early in his trek, but as the time moves on the ease of which I can cover the loss of this foreigner flies further from my grasp. Certainly, if he has already sent letters of his arrival in Bistritz, I am not blind that suspicion of murder that would come upon me if he were to disappear now. Even if it is hardly the first, it would be a poor picture to stain a newly clean record. But he *writes*. And there are ways to make these writings of his useful to me.

And then here dear Jonathan wanders my halls like a ghost, crawling up from my past. He wails like one too, in such a way that it almost breaks my heart to hear. But why — I ask? Why is this silent pleading suddenly painful when I had called on him expecting this to end in bloodshed? I fear he has become understanding of his situation — even if only lightly — and has begun to scheme against me for it. It would be wise for me to dread this, yes? So I have warned him — with civility — to avoid those places in which he has already been forbidden to go. A reminder, in case my first words were lost to him. There is an ache in my chest at the dread of cutting his life shorter than is necessary. Though now I wonder how long I will consider *necessity* when the tool has already outlived expectation? I wonder if I am thinking in terms of necessity at all, anymore — or if I am acting on compulsion.

There is danger in these uncertain thoughts.

I wonder, now, where they have come from after all this time?

Finally, an estimation; 16ᵗʰ of May. — O', I do not understand! This fury; this anger; I am teaming with life and fire, curling at the thought of these creatures I called women whom I am loathe to see lest I break them by their teeth! I told them their time would come — and I have not lied! But they looked at me, knelt over him like *wolves.* Worse than wolves with their teeth bared over his throat which I have yet even to scar myself. Had I not warned him, had I not commanded *them? —*

"You yourself never loved; you never love!" She cried to me, and I felt nothing but the strangling smoke of rage in my lungs as I coughed out my pitiful replies in a way they are too young to have ever heard me yell.

I warned him. And yet why did I not let him suffer the consequences of this defiance?

Later. — As I return to my chambers, I have calmed.

I stole Jonathan away from the women, doing with them what I must and jamming the door after the dreadful ordeal. If they are to act like wolves, they will be caged like them until I am ready once again for their presences.

He slept so soundly in his shock; stunned in a fearful silence. He even clung to me like a babe, pulling his face into my shirt and finding comfort in a way that I can only assume meant he did not realize it was I who held him. He did not even cry. But strangely the thought sticks in my mind of a time where this clinging of his might have been aware and deliberate, like lovers of old. Ay, but it is no time I will see — I live in a truthful world — a bitter one, where his usefulness lies not clung to my breast. As the night of my escape from this valley draws closer, I feel the stirring of her people quiet into a somber day, mocking the excitement that stirs within my own newly lit soul. I see him, too, stilly quiet. I could not stand the smell of their perfumes on his shirt nor the red of their lips stained on his skin and so I washed it from him; I do hope he can forgive me of this disregard. I laid him into his bed and — *O'! The life of him.* His fingers curled around my neck as I placed him down, holding to me, and it was the fire of ash and flame that struck me motionless. I lingered, and I watched, and I wondered again if all Englishmen carried themselves in such a way or if I will be *wasting* the pleasure of this one? As his breath fell from his lips, parted like they were, I was overcome with the urge to take it from him.

I ask, now, why I must leave him at all?

I answer, knowing he would never come with me. That he cannot, or else the assurance of this travel of mine would be *negotiable.*

What a strangeness I have brought onto myself bringing life into my home?

I will think of this more, in time — I have other matters to attend to. In his coat I found a diary written with unreadable scrawlings. I understand what it was I saw, and I considered taking it as I have many of his things, but the ink on these pages was fresh and the form of it desperate. I am inclined to leave him this comfort, as it will do him more good than it will harm to me.

Est., 28th of May. — I felt the footfalls of my dear Jonathan, moving through the castle after a long morning alone in his room. He has returned once again to the study to delve into the words of my companions; what a blessing he must think it is that I have so many in his English, bare it he has not touched the Greek. He reads in a quiet innocence, not daring to face me, but I know of the mischief he has been planning as his letters have come into my possession. He has attempted to send messages out to his companions without my knowledge; what endearment! What insult. One was to Peter Hawkins and the other to this Mina, of which I cannot divine the purpose. Though I am wise to understand it is not to my benefit. I cannot blame the man, but it must be known to him that this waywardness will not stand. Not with what has come into motion since his arrival here… though he knows not the breadth of these things. As I watch my plans unfold so cleanly, his affronts have caught me in a joyous way and his presence persuades me once again to mercy, even if that persuasion is slight. So, when I entered the study to confront him of his mistake, I found myself surprised by that old aching in my chest as I watched his face twist — that aching turning to pity as he then tried to bury it from me in the dark. I have not been so amused by a guest, so fond of one such as him for many years. He had tried to make himself scarce of me, but like his God, I knew already where he had hidden after causing such an issue — and like his God, I am not angry, only saddened by these actions.

He no longer greets me either, he only looked deeper into the book he had quickly ceased to read. I wondered, and thought it too cruel to ask, what was so interesting between the lines? I sat close next to him and waited for his acknowledgment, but it never came. Instead, he forced me to speak first, for this I found it needless to rebuke him. I could feel the silence was not of defiance but horror, and maybe… just maybe, I am becoming soft in my age. I spoke, and he listened. He could feel the frustration from me, and I the fear from him.

This is good, it is wise for the dying to fear.

When I approached the subject of these letters my composure in the face of dear Jonathan broke against my judgement, against my will, which had for so long remained unbroken. At the bottom of the stack I held were the lines which he had scrawled like the scratching of a beast, the language of his journal with words which the long years of my life have somehow yet to reveal to me. The assumption of this man that he could avoid me when I have attempted such generosity in the days before his death, the pain he has caused me in this effort which was otherwise so simple — it was suddenly, and surprisingly, too much for me to bear. A new anger broke through me. I felt my face darken, and in turn, his heart quicken. I cannot deny there was an old satisfaction in the youthful cruelty of showing to him his documents and seeing the realization of failure come over him so evidently.

Dear Jonathan, you cannot hide these emotions of yours. You wear them like a sheer veil that tries in vain to conceal a face.

This is something I welcome warmly from the man; it is endearing. I hear him sob in the nights, and to-night he attempted still to keep that veil as I held the scrawled paper towards the flame and burned it. The ash coated my fingers like the red of his face, and it was strange that I could feel it, thin and *hot,* in its trueful fury.

It was another *youthful cruelty*; one I thought was lost to me in the boredom of my isolation. What a goodness this man has brought into my home that I can feel the heat of fire as he might? What a sacrifice I will be making letting him end so soon; for myself, and for this 'Mina' he writes so desperately to.

"Your letters are sacred to me." I said to him, and may it be forgiven that I had lied.

Later. — It is with indignity that I stole away into dear Jonathan's room once again — like a petty thief. But it is rare that I get to act with indignity on matters such as these and still come to a satisfactory conclusion. I am no longer young, this is true; but the spirit of youth has found me again — I surround myself with this man whom I covet, and through him, I will surround myself with a new world which has been coveted from me. Outside these ancient walls is new blood, fresh and beginning that I have yet to taste the sweetness of. Life these old eyes have yet to live! Cease my hands! Lest I allow myself to become *po-etic.*

I have, in the recent nights, made strange decisions. I am aware. I moved like a man, not through mist nor wolf nor moonlight, but with legs and hands. And with fingers that have not seen the blood of battle or the slyness of conspiracy for many years I worked through his things and took the papers which were the tools to his scheming. I too took his clothes, a traveling coat and shawl, that I will use to post his letters. The idea of walking as him, unknown, unseen, unfeared and yet something that should *be* feared excites me in a way I thought was lost.

It is almost a pity that he schemes so furiously against me and yet fails so bitterly; I have long yet been tricked and realize I miss the feeling.

It was seeing him there once again, sleeping a dreamless sleep that the compulsion to eat came over me, one I have avoided say for the babe or the peasant — I decided, if I will walk like a man, steal like one, and speak like one, might I try eating as one also? I came over him and held my hand to his face, warmth of breath coursing against my fingertips and the beating of his soul strong against the silence of mine. He moved weakly under my touch, alarmed but unwoken, and there was little debate in my mind. I fed my compulsion, and it was sweet. Sweeter than it has been for centuries, even yet still cut with the bitterness of pain. But like a man who does not gorge, I constrained myself so he would not die. I feared, at one point, he had woken as his hands moved to scratch me —but then they fell limply to the bed.

Unlike him, I do not fill. Not without death. What a forfeit there is in this emptiness; what humanity. What life I will feel in his great London when the need for constraint is simply a fancy of choice. Maybe it is the headiness of his blood that clouds me so, but there again is that aching in my chest.

30th of June. — To-night, I leave this castle. These walls which have been my home and my death for lifetimes. Much has happened and much still yet to come, but I have found myself mistaken. Blinded by the triumph which I have waited so long to attain, I thought that dear Jonathan had finally broken as in these last nights, where I can see he has come to know he will lose his life, he has only attempted half-hearted escape. I watched as he threw himself to his knees and prayed, fearing no one could hear him. Knowing this to be true. But it was in these desperate nights that he found the chambers in which I rest.

How long, I wonder, would I have let him continue?

So close to my goal — instead of acting, I *watched.* If he had dug the edge of the shovel into my throat, my chest, my heart, would I have allowed him? Had he stolen a blade, would my curiosity have let me be gored to revel in this human mistake? Would he have tried at all knowing it is partially his life that sustains me so?

But he sought for my face — and I turned from him. The pitiful way he twisted sparked fury in me, but I could not bring myself to act upon it. I saw the fear in his eyes and though I know this, to him, is no betrayal, that he has no more reason to be loyal to me, I could only feel disappointment that he would attempt such a thing as this. So instead, I bled.

Like man, I *bled.* And through blood *like man* I realized, in finality, I will live. Without him, yes. But I will be free.

Finally, undated. — I must make you rid of this matter, dear Jonathan. But I cannot do it with my own hands. I must keep promises to my children.

You have given me the spark to a greater flame, and yet, I request one last thing of you, even knowing once it is written, I am too late: do not cry for your England, not for your Mina, and not for your life. These things I have and will come to know.

To know them is to love them — to love them is to truly live — and to truly live is to never truly die. I have said similar to you in the past.

For as long as I live, so will you. You have aided in something larger than yourself; I hope you can take comfort in this fact. I do. Know that it pains me leave you to this fate, but it would kill me to risk having never acted.

I will be to Carfax. I thank you. I *thank* you.

Your friend,

Dracula.

Hollyn Parsons *(She/Him)* is a new pen on the horror scene. Living in Ashland, Kentucky, but raised traveling, books - the fantastic, the horrific, and the classic - were her closest companions on the road. (Who better to roadtrip with than Dorian Gray or Mr. Harker himself?) A lifelong lover of the horrifying, she strives to bring to the table fresh tales and curious perspectives of the old and wicked. See her also in Fabled Collectives' *Women of the Woods.*

The Tale of the Szgany

By Daniel Dorsch

They called us scoundrels, wastrels, thieves, beggars. At night they came to our camp to buy our strong liquors by the jug and to leer at our women dancing by the fire. We told their fortunes and sold them goods which their godly village elders would disapprove of. They enjoyed having a grand time with us in the night.

But once daylight sprawled her brilliant fingers over these jagged mountains, they kicked us out and drove us away, calling us a dangerous nuisance. They called us "gypsy," ignoring our true name, the Szgany. We were a blot on their tranquil pastoral existence out here among the Carpathians, and they wanted nothing to do with us in the light of day.

What did we do? Why, we took the coins they dropped in the night, accepted our role as outcasts in the day, and moved on, welcome everywhere at night and nowhere during the day.

That was, until we met the Count.

He first came to us one cold winter evening, an old man with a proud bearing, looking to all the world like some veteran of long-forgotten wars as he leaned on a walking stick. His clothing was ancient and tattered, but it spoke of bygone wealth and power. At first glance, he seemed a pitiful figure but intriguing, so we invited him to join us around the fire.

It seemed strange at the time, but he had a presence to him that instantly made us all want to be his friend. Yes, he seemed humbler than the smallest off us, but somehow there was also an authority to him, a charisma and regal nature which reminded us of the great lords who once ruled over these mountains and drove away one invading force after another.

Intently he listened to our stories of adventure and abuses, of accusations from jealous wives whose husbands had dallied with one of our young ladies and come home with smiling faces and empty pockets, of church elders accusing us of thefts while their personal coffers mysteriously filled. He heard us tell of dogs being set on us as we hastened to pick up camp, of taverns and grocers refusing us business, of our children's empty stomachs and our men's increased desperation.

As our violins played and our young people danced in the firelight, he clapped and smiled. He gave us a small bag of gold, urged us to keep our spirits up, and promised to return.

Return he did, just as he promised. He shared stories of his own with us, but his were much more exciting. His tales were all about battles of bygone eras, told with as much vivid detail and enthusiasm as though he were there himself. Once upon a time, he said, his family slew all the enemies who threatened this country.

In the darkness, we could practically hear the clashing of swords and the singing of arrows, the ringing of battle horns and the screams of bloodthirsty legions. We could almost see the forest of enemy corpses impaled to send a grisly message to those who threatened these lands, to teach them all to fear the Order of the Dragon.

That was when we began to understand to which family this mysterious old man belonged. The people of the area still whispered with a type of frightened reverence about The Impaler, the man who threw back armies of invaders and who committed unspeakable acts upon his enemies, both within and without his kingdom. Bloodshed was an art to him, and he was a genius at inspiring fear.

This Impaler, he sounded like a butcher. He sounded like a terror.

He sounded like a good person to have on your side.

At first, we kept our friendship with the old man out of a sort of curiosity, and because he seemed to know how to make gold appear. Despite our own desperate situation, nobody ever gave a thought to robbing him or murdering him for his money. That just was not an option with the Count. He would come to us at night, only ever at night, and he would always leave behind a reminder of why he was a good friend.

Over time, strange and wonderful things began to happen. A man who claimed one of our children stole from him suddenly turned up dead, all evidence of the theft gone.

Another man had indulged in the pleasures of the night with us, but then refused to pay. He called us "scum lower than dogs." Only the next day, he was found mauled to death by wolves in the forest on the edge of town. Meanwhile, the money he owed us appeared suddenly in our own humble treasury.

A churchman who called for the townspeople to drive us "heathens" away was found blithering and terrified in his own churchyard one morning, and the subject of our expulsion quickly dropped.

Only a fool would fail to notice that our remarkable good fortune coincided with the appearance of the Count, and we let him know that he could rely on us for anything he needed. He would hold us to that promise. When a beautiful young woman with dark hair disappeared one night from a nearby village, we knew where she went, but nobody breathed a word. When another disappeared a few months later, again we said nothing. Even when the fair child of a local boyar disappeared and her father launched a full-scale hunt which promised a rich reward for her safe return, still we said nothing.

But we noticed how the Count seemed to wither on certain days when all was normal in the local villages, and how he seemed revitalized and almost even youthful when people went missing. We knew that our friend was responsible, but we had absolutely no intention of exposing him. And somehow we knew that he was aware of this, and his reaction was only increased generosity.

It was after several years, many bags of gold, and numerous missing people that we began to realize that our quiet benefactor was planning something that would require our help. The first sign was when he invited us to his home, a ruined castle in the mountains where he allowed us to encamp in the courtyards and use the old embattlements to shelter in. There was a loyalty, a generosity between us, the outcast people, and him, the long-forgotten nobleman.

Yes, we had begun to realize just who exactly our friend was, and we only respected him more for it. After all, the only difference between a monster and a rich gentleman is that a monster is honest. Even the wolves seemed to become our friends because of the Count, as they refused to attack us, and even protected our comings and goings, especially when we traveled on business for him.

Whatever our friend's plan, we were only too happy to help. Soon it became apparent that this involved London, England. He had us go out into the daytime, the one time he did not seem active, and fetch him all the books and maps we could which pertained to that city. Sometimes we bought these or traded for them. Other times we just stole them. It mattered not to us or to him. A rich man takes what he wants because he can afford anything. Poor tramps like us take what we can get because it's the only way to survive. We're all thieves, really.

The arrival of the young Englishman marked the stimulus for the Count's plan to finally spring into motion. If we weren't so anxious to ensure our friend's success, we might have felt pity for the poor boy. He was a lamb to slaughter, just like all those maidens and children who disappeared into the Count's castle over the years. The only difference was that he clearly had some part to play in this new London venture.

In any case, our loyalty to the Count was much stronger than any pity we had for the young fool, so naturally when he tried to pay one of us to deliver letters for him behind the Count's back, we immediately handed those letters over. One shudders to think what awful future he faces, locked away in the fastness of the old fortress.

We could guess what the Count needed from us, when he arranged for the large boxes to be brought to the castle. Still no questions were necessary when he ordered them filled with dirt from the castle grounds, Transylvanian soil. It was a simple enough task, just like the arrangement of carts to haul the boxes down to the port. What is a little labor between friends, after all?

Demeter, the ship is named, a reference to the gods of old, now carrying this strange cargo. Perhaps it is a godlike power which now sails aboard it, bound for the heart of merry old England.

A god, perhaps, or a demon.

Whatever he is, it matters little to us. When we were a pariah, he took us in. He paid us, fed us, gave us work and protected us.

He is our friend.

As the *Demeter* prepares to set sail, a terrible storm is coming, bringing with it all the darkness of this strange and haunted country. A power is coming which mere mortals cannot hope to defeat.

The Count is coming. May God have mercy on London, and all who live there.

Daniel Dorsch lives in Capon Bridge, West Virginia, a quiet and mysterious little village in the haunted hills of the Shenandoah Valley. He works as a Special Education English teacher during the day and spends his evenings with his family and his thoughts, channeling them into creativity whenever he can.

Norsemen Cruise Line

By Henry Herz

Yes, Mr. Torgersen. I shall embark on the next ship departing San Diego with my assistant. Thank you for trusting my firm with this sensitive matter." I hung up the phone. Easing back in my black and onyx Herman Miller Aeron desk chair, I surveyed the framed accolades mounted on my office's ebony board and batten paneling. "Well, this should be interesting," I mused.

"What's that, sir?" asked Ray, entering the room carrying a carton of case files into my office. As always, my muscular assistant's wrinkled tie matched his disheveled blond hair.

I pointed to the phone. "I just spoke with the head of security for Norsemen Cruise Line. He wishes me to investigate the higher than usual incidence of passenger disappearances on their San Diego to Mazatlán cruises."

Ray's wiry eyebrows rose. "Higher than *usual*, sir?"

"Yes, apparently cruise lines regularly lose passengers." I pulled up an incident report from Torgersen on my computer. "Most of the MIAs are simply those who fail to return to the ship in time before it departs a port call. But cruise ships also regularly experience unexplained absences. I imagine some drunken passengers jump overboard for a thrill or inadvertently tumble overboard at night… or are tossed overboard by jealous husbands."

Ray set down the document carton. "With all respect sir, why isn't the cruise line engaging a traditional private investigator or the police?"

I stood and straightened my blood red Hermès silk tie. "They have not contacted the authorities because they do not wish for this problem to become public. They are doubly concerned because the percentage of missing who are female has risen precipitously. Norsemen Cruise Line contacted me due to my reputation for resolving paranormal investigations with discretion."

I rotated my computer monitor so Ray could see. "Ship security cameras have noted some odd-looking folks on deck at night." I brought up a screen shot of one such man, zooming in. The passenger's narrow balding head featured a downturned, thick-lipped mouth, small ears, flat nose, and watery-blue bulging eyes. Yellow hairs straggled in irregular patches from grayish cheeks. Scabrous folds lined both sides of his neck.

Ray bent over the screen for a closer look. "No crime in being ugly, sir."

"Agreed, so long as one is well-dressed and manicured."

A week later, Ray and I boarded the Norsemen cruise ship Demeter in San Diego, he via the gangway and myself by a less conventional method. I lay within my antique mahogany steamer trunk. In addition to holding my person, the capacious baggage differed from others in that it locked from both the outside and the inside… and dirt from my native Transylvania lined the bottom. Judiciously sipping the blood of successive generations of Renfields, I no longer needed to stalk strangers. I now spent my time challenging my intellect by preventing tragedies instead of inflicting them — a vampiric detective.

I remained fully awake, regaining strength from the Transylvanian soil as I listened to the sounds of a forklift carry me aboard. As Dracula, I possess many powers, but nonetheless require assistance with certain activities, boarding a ship being one of them.

Chatty baggage handlers loaded me onto an elevator, which raised me to the lobby of the thirteenth deck. Someone rolled me to my stateroom and knocked on the door. "Your luggage," announced a handler with a pleasing Norwegian accent.

The stateroom door unlocked. "Ah, come in," said Ray, as faithful a Renfield as any of his forebears. "Please set all the luggage there."

The handler deposited our suitcases before lifting one end of my heavy trunk.

"Here…" Ray must have paused to read a name tag, "Øystein. Let me help you with that."

"Thanks. There's no better feeling than doing backbreaking work for someone else for low pay," Øystein joked. He and Ray moved my steamer. A pause. "Ah, very kind of you," he added, likely in response to a generous tip from Ray. The stateroom door clicked shut.

Ray unlatched the outside of my trunk, while I unlocked the inside. I emerged to stretch and survey the amenities of our opulent penthouse. The crystal fixtures sparkled. The marble countertops gleamed. No detail had been overlooked. Towel origami shaped like an elephant adorned my bed.

"I'll fix you the usual, sir." Ray strode to the well-stocked wet bar and mixed me a Bloody Mary. He brought me my drink and the Demeter's floor plans provided by the cruise line.

"Thank you, Ray." I nodded after taking a tentative taste. "Ah, Vikingfjord vodka. Lovely. Did you know they distill it using water from the Jostedalsbreen glacier in southwestern Norway?" I stepped onto our private balcony to enjoy the view. Contrary to common belief, sunlight restricts my powers but does not destroy me. I appreciated Hollywood unknowingly exaggerating my vulnerability. Raising my glass, I toasted, "To Bela Lugosi and Christopher Lee."

I finished my cocktail as the Demeter slipped its moorings and sailed from San Diego Harbor. Flipping through the floor plans, I committed them to my eidetic memory. "Now, let us familiarize ourselves with the deck layouts first-hand."

"Very good, sir." Ray handed me my ivory-handled walking cane. I looked like a middle-aged man and needed no crutch, but I found it prudent to portray myself as frailer than I really was.

We observed the crew and passengers as we strolled the decks. A cruise ship is truly a microcosm of humanity, a floating festival of tropes. Joy was written on the face of many. Giggling children bent their bodies beneath limbo sticks. The newly married posed for professional photographs. Silver-haired couples smiled while playing shuffleboard.

Also present in full measure were the seven deadly sins. I could practically smell them. Sloth: Fair-skinned passengers sunned themselves, bossing around waitstaff rather than moving for themselves. Gluttony: We passed a buffet where people stuffed themselves beyond all need and drank themselves into a stupor. Greed: Passengers in the casino lost money they could ill afford, caught up in the rapturous pursuit of wealth. Wrath: A drunken man shoved another, leading to fisticuffs. "Notice how one kind of sin can spawn another, Ray?"

He nodded. "Yes, sir. That bikini contest perfectly illustrates your point."

Pride: sexy women flaunted their bodies for attention. Envy: beer-gutted men scowled, wishing their wives looked like the contestants. Lust: a handsome waiter led an eager passenger by the hand for an elicit coupling.

"The full rainbow of iniquity, masking the greater evil of those we seek." *Ah, humanity, swimming in sin. Who are you to judge me?*

T he cruise line had informed the captain of our assignment and arranged for me and Ray to eat at his table during the late dinner time slot.

The captain, a uniformed man with blue eyes, a full head of hair, and a neatly trimmed Van Dyke, addressed our table warmly. Like the baggage handler, he spoke English with a Norwegian accent. "Welcome everyone. I'm Captain Conradi." He indicated his epaulette. "But please call me Kåre." He pointed to a uniformed man to his right. "And this is the cruise director, Trond Fausa."

The slender, brown-haired mustached man nodded. "Thanks, Captain. I arranged the on-board entertainment. That includes the Norwegian band, Grand Island, playing in the dance hall." He glanced at a couple seated to my right. "And we are lucky to have the hilarious stand-up comedy duo of Marian Ottesen and Nils Jørgen Kaalstad."

Marian had wavy blonde hair, a lovely white throat, and a smile that lit up the room. Jovial Nils's curved spine made him appear chubby, but he had great facial features.

The cruise director added, "I also arranged the art installation on the sun deck this afternoon."

A diner two seats to my left, who had been imbibing a constant stream of Aquavit shots said, "I didn't much care for it."

Trond forced a smile. "This is good. Because art is supposed to provoke and challenge, create debate, even disgust."

Ray spoke up. "Kåre, can you tell us why the seating arrangements change each meal?"

The captain gave him a broad smile, clearly appreciating the change in topic. "It's very important not to get these cliques on-board. And who knows, maybe some strong new friendships can develop."

Fortunately, our appetizers arrived, obviating the need for further banal conversation. I ate solely for courtesy's sake, since I only derive nourishment from human blood.

Ray attacked with gusto the Norwegian *brunost* brown cheese, *Sunnmørsbrød* rye bread, and *sursild* pickled herring. But when the unexpectedly gelatinous *lutefisk* entrée was served, the barely concealed revulsion on his face nearly prompted a chuckle from me.

"Ray, do you feel like stretching your legs?"

He nodded with alacrity, and we excused ourselves. "Thank you, sir."

We took in the night air, admiring the stars. I usually feel old among mortals, but the stars' vast age reminded me how young I truly am.

Once we reached the privacy of our penthouse, Ray raised an arm, exposing his wrist. "Are you thirsty, sir?"

"Thank you, Ray, but I am fine. I think I shall patrol the passageways."

I wandered for several hours, encountering no strange-looking men nor illegal acts, only numerous examples of human moral turpitude.

Before returning to my stateroom, I checked one last compartment — a housekeeping storage room. Toilet paper rolls, bottles of cleaning supplies, and towels littered the floor — far more than might be expected from a drunken couple's wildly energetic fornication. Though none of the bottles had spilled, I caught a faint whiff of a chemical scent, but could not place it.

I hustled to the ship's bridge, requesting the officer in charge convey a message to the captain to conduct a passenger head count on the morrow.

The next day, we docked at Cabo San Lucas. I spent the daylight hours in my steamer trunk, revitalizing.

When I rose in mid-afternoon, Ray greeted me with a grim face. "Sir, we received a message from Captain Conradi. Two passengers, a man and woman in their twenties, are missing."

I nodded. "A tragedy for them, but a confirmation that villains are aboard the ship."

The Demeter put out to sea just before dinner time.

The full moon rose. Back in my stateroom, I checked my platinum and black enamel Patek Philippe 5088/100P Calatrava wristwatch. "Midnight approaches. I think I shall conduct a covert aerial patrol for a few hours."

Ray nodded. "Very good, sir." He slid open a window.

I changed into my winged form, flitting out of the penthouse and into the night. As a bat, my vision lacked the sharpness and color discernment of human eyes, but possessed excellent light sensitivity. And, of course, I had its superb hearing.

Silent and nearly invisible, I circled above the open decks. The number of passengers outside diminished with time, except for a brief surge after one o'clock, when the ship bars closed, disgorging drunks destined to make out or pass out.

Eventually, the decks had cleared. At least until two figures carrying bulky bundles emerged from a doorway astern and slinked along the starboard promenade deck toward the bow. Their movement betrayed none of the unsteadiness associated with inebriation. I drifted closer and discovered both men possessed the same odd facial features as in the photographs shared with me by cruise line security.

The pair halted amidships. The taller man with a satchel withdrew a long slender rope knotted at one-meter intervals. He tied one end to the railing and released the rope overboard into the water far below.

Interesting.

I descended for a closer look at where the rope trailed in the ocean, buffeted by gusts of Pacific Ocean air. The moon cast queer reflections on the smooth surface below me. Suddenly, I saw sparkling. *Something is disturbing the bioluminescent plankton.*

With only a slight churning to mark its rise to the surface, a webbed, clawed hand slid into view above the cold waters.

A figure seized the rope and emerged from the depths, clad only in the still-twinkling water dripping off it. It climbed with a spastic lurching both disturbing and suggestive of great strength. The creature, for I could not bring myself to consider it a man, looked like a disturbingly humanoid fish-frog. Shiny gray-green covered its warped body, except for a white abdomen and scaly back ridges. The fish-like head, supported by a thick, gilled neck, featured dead bulbous eyes.

I ascended as the hideous creature hauled itself up and over the rail with long gangly limbs. I circled silently twenty feet above the trio, wrapped in darkness.

The two men bowed. One pulled up and coiled the rope, while the other unfolded his bundle. He reverently wrapped a large blanket around the creature to mask its hideous appearance, whispering "Please follow us to room 8130, Lord."

Lord? I recognized 8130 to be the starboard-most stateroom at the stern of the eighth deck. I flitted through to the corresponding window. Open to admit the salty sea air, the window's bottom edge offered me a hidden perch. I dangled upside-down outside the opening, hidden from view.

Seeping from the opening like unseen poisonous effluvia, the nearly insufferable fetor of rotting organic matter almost made me gag.

Minutes later, the stateroom door opened. The light switched on, followed by moist slapping sounds.

Footsteps? Bending at the waist, I raised my head, risking a brief glance to confirm it was the ichthyic intruder and his two guides. On a table lay an oval platter of decomposing fish, clearly the source of the putrescent miasma.

"Refreshment, Lord?"

A deep grunt and disgusting slurps followed. "Ah, delicciouss." The creature wheezed between words, as if unused to breathing air. Between that and the sibilance, its voice was as repellent as its appearance.

"What preparationss have you made to ssecure more human bridess?"

"Lord, we suggest tomorrow night after we depart Puerto Vallarta. The cruise line will assume any missing people failed to re-board the ship before departure. After the bars close, drunken passengers often mate in the ship's nooks and crannies. We'll chloroform them, tossing the males overboard. We have a satellite phone to call the speedboat trailing the cruise ship. We'll lower your new brides onto the speedboat."

"Mosst ssatissfactory. Anything elsse?"

The speaker cleared his throat, conveying reluctance. "Well, Lord, our informant tells us there's a supernatural detective aboard, possibly a vampire or werewolf. We're scouring the ship for suitable weapons."

Damn. They must have bribed a Norsemen security employee.

The creature hissed. "Take whatever sstepss are neccessary, but get uss thosse bridess!"

I released my grip on the window edge, gliding into the night and back to my room, where I returned to my human form. "Bring me my tomes, Ray."

"Of course, sir." He set a small wooden travel case on the tabletop, unlocking it to reveal the usual arcane reference books — Codex Monstra et Carmina, Spate's Catalog, Tobin's Spirit Guide, The Necronomicon, and so on. As I flipped through vellum pages yellowed with age, Ray served a Bloody Mary.

"Interesting," I said after thirty minutes of searching.

"Sir?"

I motioned Ray over, pointing at an illustration depicting a creature resembling the one that had emerged from the ocean. "According to this codex, that is a Deep One. They worship the gargantuan Old Gods, Dagon and Hydra. Their blasphemous matings with humans produce hybrids, like the fellow photographed by Norsemen security. I overheard their plans to kidnap passengers tomorrow night. But I shall thwart them."

T he following midnight, I changed my form to a fine mist, floating into the ship's ventilation system to begin a time-consuming patrol of potential drunken tryst locations: meeting rooms, empty dining rooms, cafés, and restaurants, covered lifeboats, even golf cages and empty bowling alleys. After the bars shut at one o'clock, I checked the darkened watering holes as well — the champagne and wine bar, the martini and cocktail bar, and the beer and whiskey bar. I began a second circuit in the early morning quiet.

Muffled sounds of a struggle emanated from behind the door of a public restroom near the stern of the sixth deck. I drifted into the corridor and assumed my human corporeal form, fully clothed (I possess the power but not the scientific explanation for this ability). I eased open the door.

A partially dressed (or undressed, if one is an optimist) couple lay unconscious on the tile floor. Two Deep One hybrids knelt over them holding chloroform-soaked rags.

The hybrid closer to me leapt to his feet, drew a long silver knife from a wrist sheath, and lunged. I dodged his repeated thrusts with my supernatural reflexes. "Is this futile exercise really necessary?" When my appeal to reason failed, I changed tactics and let him strike me. Silver may be lethal against werewolves, but mundane weapons caused me no harm. He stabbed me twice more. His obstinate rudeness exhausted my patience. I punched him in the face so hard his skull cracked.

He crumpled to the floor.

I turned to the second hybrid to see if he had learned from his comrade's experience.

While he had not drawn a weapon, he held a mobile phone. Instead of attacking me, he had FaceTimed my brief fight.

Damn. In a blur, I seized his phone in one hand and his neck with my other hand. I squeezed until both broke.

I knelt and administered aid to the unconscious would-be lovers. Before I could rouse them, three more hybrids burst into the room.

More? No matter.

I stood. "Gentlemen, much as I appreciate an opportunity for exercise, this has grown tiresome." I pointed at the hybrid corpses. "Look at your colleagues. Surely, your hybrid genetics have not eliminated your sense of self-preservation."

Instead of being swayed by my wit or intimidated by the violence I had wrought, they offered me only grim smiles. Rather than blades, they yanked crosses or garlic cloves from their jacket pockets.

Fortune favors the prepared, I mused. For on this matter, pop culture representations were regrettably accurate. I cannot abide crosses or garlic, and the hybrids blocked the room's only exit.

Two of them forced me into a corner. The third tucked away his garlic, knelt, and gathered the unconscious woman in his arms. He stood and shuffled laboriously out of the room, ignoring my snarled threat to tear him apart.

A sharp crack outside the room preceded the sound of bodies collapsing to the deck.

The hybrids menacing me shared a glance. "Go see what happened," ordered one.

The other obeyed while his companion kept his eyes locked on me.

Crack.

Ray charged into the room, swinging my ebony cane. He struck the hybrid's right wrist, who winced in pain, dropping the cross.

With no defense against the painful cane strikes, the hybrid panicked. He drew a knife from a wrist sheath.

I was on him in a blur before he could lunge at Ray, snapping his neck like a dry twig. "Thank you very much for the timely assistance, Ray. We should—"

The Deep One lurched into the room like a grotesque frog, knocking Ray sideways into a wall with a sweep of its gangly arm. The cane clattered into a corner — the corner into which the garlic-brandishing Deep One backed me as it chanted in a baleful language, "Ph'nglui mglw'nafh Dagon R'lyeh wgah'nagl fhtagn."

What are you saying? Did you kill Ray?

"Iä Dagon cf'ayak'vulgtmm, vugtlagln vulgtmm."

My feet rooted to the floor. *A magical spell?*

The hideous creature barked, "Interfering fool! No one may hinder the sservantss of Dagon. I pinned you in placce like a moth. Now you will watch me end your puny asssisstant, contemplating your ressponssibility for hiss awful fate until you wither away without your native ssoil." It stepped toward Ray, putrid drool dripping from its thick-lipped maw. Wrapping its clawed webbed hands around Ray's neck, it lifted him off the floor and squeezed.

Ray awakened, his eyes wide in pain and terror. He kicked and flailed to no avail against the creature's strength.

Although I could not move my feet, I retained control of the rest of my body. With my supernatural speed, I squatted and grabbed my cane from the floor. I drew the narrow, hidden sword from the cane and hurled it at the Deep One with all my might and fury.

The blade pierced its head, tacking it to the wall… dare I say, like a moth. A putrid green ichor dripped down the creature's head. Death cancelled the caster's spell.

Fortune favors the prepared.

I rushed to Ray, who had collapsed onto the floor. Relief rushed over me as he drew a breath.

Probably a concussion and a fractured left clavicle.

"Rest, Ray, while I clean up the mess. Then I shall carry you to the ship's medical center."

And notify Security.

It turned out that in his zeal to aid me, my beefy assistant had shattered both of his opponents' skulls, so Norsemen Cruise Line had no untidy loose ends in the form of witnesses. I suspect the corpses of the Deep One and hybrids were tossed overboard that night, perhaps even by the ever cheerful Øystein. I wondered about the appropriate tip for disposing of bodies.

Suffice it to say, Captain Conradi had the crew treat us like royalty for the remainder of the cruise — no luxury spared, no gratuitously indulgent request unfulfilled.

Payment to my firm, Tepes Investigations, included a fat bonus to encourage our continued discretion.

Author's Note

The Norwegian foods and drinks mentioned are authentic. The named Norwegian characters are those of real-life actors from the hilarious Netflix historical comedy, *Norsemen*, of which this story is a respectful parody. Any resemblance to an actual cruise line is purely coincidental. The Demeter, of course, is an homage to the doomed ship traveling to England in Bram Stoker's novel, *Dracula*.

Spate's Catalog and *Tobin's Spirit Guide* are winks at the Ghostbusters movie. The Necronomicon is a fictional book imagined by H.P. Lovecraft. Deep One and Deep One hybrid creatures appeared in Lovecraft's stories *Dagon* (1919) and *The Shadow Over Innsmouth* (1931). Since seaweed can naturally produce chloroform, it seemed a logical weapon for the Deep Ones.

Henry Herz's speculative fiction short stories include *Out, Damned Virus* (Daily Science Fiction), *Bar Mitzvah on Planet Latke* (Coming of Age, Albert Whitman & Co.), *The Magic Backpack* (Metastellar), *Unbreakable* (Musing of the Muses, Brigid's Gate Press), *A Vampire, an Astrophysicist, and a Mother Superior Walk Into a Basilica* (Three Time Travelers Walk Into…, Fantastic Books), *The Case of the Murderous Alien* (Spirit Machine, Air and Nothingness Press), *The Ghosts of Enerhodar* (Literally Dead, Alienhead Press), *Maria & Maslow* (Highlights for Children), and *A Proper Party* (Ladybug Magazine). He's written twelve picture books, including the critically acclaimed *I Am Smoke*. www.henryherz.com

Elizabeth

A One Act Play

By Gerard J. Waggett

Dramatis Personae

Dracula
Elizabeth Bathory
Court Officer
Guard #1
Guard #2
Guard #3

Setting: Late August night in Elizabeth Bathory's bedchamber. The room contains a bed, a stuffed chair, a writing desk, a bureau, and an armoire. There is a fireplace and a window, but there are no mirrors on any of the walls.

The door to the bedroom has been replaced with a brick wall. One quarter of the way down the wall is an open slat through which meals can be passed to Elizabeth.

When the play opens, ELIZABETH, 54 years old, is lying on top of her bed, fanning herself. DRACULA is onstage but hidden in the shadows beneath the window.

A bat begins flapping its wings outside Elizabeth's window, then seems to disappear. Dracula emerges from the shadows.

Elizabeth pulls herself into a sitting position on the bed.

ELIZABETH
You came.

Dracula walks over to the brick wall and slaps his hand against it.

DRACULA
The rumors have not been exaggerated.

ELIZABETH
(Stands up)
I have been sent to my room like a naughty child.

Mouth of COURT OFFICER appears at the slat in the wall.

COURT OFFICER
Countess Elizabeth Bathory de Ecsed, for the crimes of murder and torture in numbers beyond calculation or comprehension, you have been sentenced to spend the remainder of your days under house arrest, isolated from society, among whom you no longer deserve the right to walk.

Court Officer's mouth disappears from the slat.

ELIZABETH
According to popular opinion, I have been shown undue lenience because of my title. The public wanted to see me hang alongside my servants.

DRACULA
It is never good politics to let the masses see nobility executed.

(Surveys the room)

No mirrors.

ELIZABETH

That was the first detail I noticed in your castle. It confirmed all my suspicions.

DRACULA

I had suspicions about you as well, but I never anticipated your true motive for wanting to meet such a distant relative.

ELIZABETH

My research into eternal youth kept bringing me back to the vampire legend. Coupled with those reports from Transylvania, peasant girls found drained of blood, I cannot believe that I was the first one to connect you—

DRACULA

(interrupting)

You weren't.

ELIZABETH

That's right. The Vatican knows. How did you phrase it? They consider you "good for business." How many conversions do you think they've sold based on your fear of the cross?

DRACULA

It is not fear.

ELIZABETH

Would you prefer the term "weakness"?

DRACULA
(Still surveying room)
Do you honestly prefer this room over the
end of a rope?

ELIZABETH
I wouldn't be here if you had made me
one of you.

DRACULA
A wise general does not arm potential
enemies.

ELIZABETH
Dear Cousin, you miss my potential as an
ally.

DRACULA
You would eventually betray me.

ELIZABETH
Haven't I kept your secret all these
decades? Haven't I honored my promise
not to approach another vampire?

DRACULA
Only because you knew I would find out
and destroy you.

ELIZABETH
I was surprised you didn't kill me that
night when you caught me with your
wives.

DRACULA
The disappearance of a noble woman
would have invited unwelcome scrutiny.

That's a lesson you should have learned. Nobody in power cared about the peasants you were butchering.

ELIZABETH
I have much to learn from you.

GUARD #1
(Voice is heard on other side of wall.)
Stop talking to yourself!

DRACULA
Servants speak to you like that?

ELZABETH
My guards have all been carefully selected, every single one of them related to one of my victims. Brothers, cousins, fiancés. Even a father.

GUARD #2's eyes appear in the slat. They take in the whole room.

GUARD #2
A cozy little room you have here. A comfortable chair to sit on. A comfortable bed to sleep in at night. Much too nice for a monster like you.

ELIZABETH
Who are you?

GUARD #2
They say you peeled the skin off my daughter's face because you were jealous of her beauty.

ELIZABETH
I was probably just curious.

GUARD #2
She was beautiful. And young. Not ugly
and wrinkled like you. Go on, take a good
look at yourself.

Guard #2 disappears from the slat.

ELIZABETH
(to Dracula)
That was the day I smashed my mirror.

DRACULA
Are all the guards like that?

ELIZABETH
Some are worse. The ways they have
defiled my food …

DRACULA
So who posted that letter you sent?

ELIZABETH
It took years, but I finally found someone
whose greed outweighed family loyalty.

Elizabeth removes a letter and a gold bracelet from her writing
desk. She brings them over to the wall. GUARD #3's face can
now be seen through the slat.

GUARD #3
Is that gold?

ELIZABETH
Pure gold.

Guard #3 reaches his hand through the slat to grab the bracelet. Elizabeth holds it just beyond his reach.

> ELIZABETH
> (cont'd)
> Swear that you will post this letter today.

> GUARD #3
> I swear.

> ELIZABETH
> Swear on your sister's grave.

> GUARD #3
> I swear on Lydia's grave.

Elizabeth passes the letter and the bracelet through the slat. Guard #3 disappears from view.

> ELIZABETH
> (to Dracula)
> I planned to use this favor against him. He would not want the other guards knowing that he helped me.

> DRACULA
> What would they have done?

> ELIZABETH
> Exactly what they did.

A plate is passed through the slat. On top of it is a man's severed hand with Elizabeth's bracelet around its wrist.

Elizabeth takes the bracelet off the wrist.She licks at the dried blood stains, then pushes the plate and hand back through the slat.

ELIZABETH
(cont'd)
I was afraid that the letter had not been
posted.But here you are.

DRACULA
I want to hear about this ritual you
discovered.

ELIZABETH
With my help, the cross will never again
bring you to your knees.

DRACULA
Nothing brings me to my knees.

ELIZABETH
Even a child holding the smallest cross—

DRACULA
(Cutting her off)
Where did you discover this secret?

ELIZABETH
My blood crimes attracted the attention of
the Vatican. They sent a vampire hunter
here to see if I was one of the undead.

DRACULA
And he shared the ritual with you?

ELIZABETH
Not willingly.
(short pause)
It was the first time I had ever tortured
someone for reasons beyond my own
amusement.

DRACULA
How can you be sure he wasn't lying?

ELIZABETH
He took his own life after revealing the secret.

DRACULA
What does this ritual entail?

ELIZABETH
I will share that information after you and I have shared blood.

DRACULA
My feelings have not changed.

ELIZABETH
Then I will carry the secret with me to Hell.

DRACULA
(Grabs Elizabeth by the wrist)
You are not the only one adept at torture.

ELIZABETH
I would welcome that as relief from the endless boredom in this room.

Dracula lets go of Elizabeth's wrist.

ELIZABETH
(cont'd)
Imagine being able to pluck the cross out of a victim's hand. Imagine the shock on their faces. Sorry, the church cannot pro-

tect you. Tell me that's not worth risking your fears.

DRACULA

I'm not afraid of you, Elizabeth, not as you are now, and not of what you will become.

ELIZABETH

That sounds like we have reached an understanding.

DRACULA

Understand this. If the ritual does not work, I will destroy you.

Dracula opens his mouth, but Elizabeth steps back away from him.

DRACULA
(cont'd)
There is no ritual, is there?

ELIZABETH

No, there is. The vampire hunter admitted so. He also revealed that it needs to be performed by a priest who has lost his faith. Unfortunately, he killed himself before revealing everything.

DRACULA

You lying—

ELIZABETH
(Interrupting)
We can find another hunter who knows the secret. Together, we can get the information out of him.

> DRACULA
>
> You have lured me here on a fool's errand.

> ELIZABETH
>
> Cousin—

> DRACULA
>
> You will die in this room.

> ELIZABETH
>
> (Throws herself at Dracula's feet)
> When I first came to you, I was driven by vanity. Now it's a matter of survival.

> DRACULA
>
> (Yanks Elizabeth back to her feet)
> Your survival shames our family. You are mocked by servants, forced to eat their filth—

> ELIZABETH
>
> (Interrupting)
> Give me the power to avenge myself, to avenge our family honor.

Dracula bites Elizabeth on the neck.

> ELIZABETH
>
> (cont'd)
> Thank you.

Elizabeth rips at Dracula's shirt trying to expose his chest. Dracula swats her hands away.

> ELIZABETH
>
> (cont'd)
> I thought …

DRACULA

I'm doing what you should have done the
first day they sealed you into this room.

ELIZABETH
(Rubbing hands together)
My hands have gone cold. The girls, some
complained about cold hands when I was
draining them. They complained shortly
before—
(Runs to wall, sticks hands through the slat)
Guard! I need a doctor.My hands are cold.

GUARD #1
(Voice)
It's nothing, Mistress. Go lie down.

ELIZABETH
(Pulls hands back through the slat)
Your fiancée did not die a virgin.

DRACULA

He's right, Elizabeth. You need to get into
bed.

ELIZABETH

No.

DRACULA

You don't want them finding you on the
floor.

Dracula guides Elizabeth into the bed.

ELIZABETH

You'll never discover the ritual without
me. You'll always be helpless …

Elizabeth closes her eyes.

Dracula seems to disappear right before a bat flies out of the room via the slat in the wall.

SOUND OF SCUFFLE OUTSIDE THE ROOM

SOUND OF A HEAD BEING SMASHED REPEATEDLY AGAINST THE BRICK WALL.

Blood trickles down the wall from the slat.

CURTAIN

Gerard J Waggett has published eleven books on soap opera trivia. In the past two years, his detective fiction has been read in *Mystery Magazine*. Mr. Waggett teaches first year writing at Suffolk University in Boston's Beacon Hill as well as a course in supernatural literature at Bunker Hill Community College, where he also developed an honors course on vampires. This past spring, sequart.com published Mr. Waggett's retrospective on *Marvel's Tomb of Dracula* comic book. He is a two day *Jeopardy!* champion.

The Night Museum

By Jessica Gleason

Dracula @OGDrac
I'm Drac. Like Dracula, bloodsucker, creature of the night. #hitwitter

Dracula @OGDrac
Ugh. The internet is worse than 1440s Wallachia. You people will believe that the world is flat, but not that vampires exist. #micdrop

Dracula @OGDrac
Yes, I am dramatic. I'm an old old man. #getoffmylawn

Dracula @OGDrac
Ok, let's try this again. It's me, Dracula, and I am so bored. There are cows outside. They aren't tasty or good conversationalists. Dazzle me. #hitwitter

Dracula @OGDrac
I feel like I'm screaming into the void. Am I screaming into the void? #helloooo

Dracula @OGDrac
So, I'm here living in the suburban Midwest. I needed a change of pace, but the night life here is desolate. At least we have this beautiful lake.

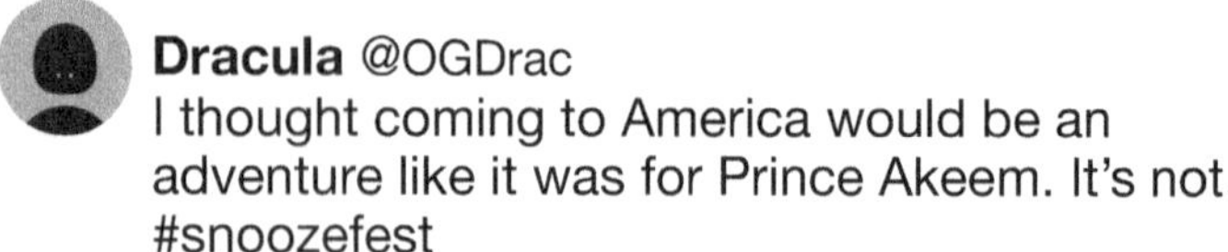

Dracula @OGDrac
I thought coming to America would be an adventure like it was for Prince Akeem. It's not. #snoozefest

Dracula @OGDrac
What you don't think vampires like Eddie Murphy? Spoiler alert: we do.

Dracula @OGDrac
Look, yes, I've done some terrible things. Big death. Much blood. But, that was the past. I'm a modern vampire now with modern sensibilities

Dracula @OGDrac
Things haven't been great. Reinfeld and I are fighting. I need new friends. A new purpose.

Dracula @OGDrac
It snows too much here and then there's even less for a night creature to do.

Dracula @OGDrac
So, I've gone out into town. Everything shuttered before I woke except a few bars full of unsavory sorts.

Dracula @OGDrac
Skipped the bars because I don't want to get myself in trouble, but this town has a certain charm, moonlight sparkling on the frozen lake and all that.

Dracula @OGDrac
People seem to feel safe here. It's so very quaint and quiet.

Dracula @OGDrac
There have to be more people like me up there, right? Maybe you're not vampires, but you love the nightlife? You like to boogie?

Dracula @OGDrac
@gettinfiggywitit Thank you. Finally, someone who's awake. My people have arrived!

Dracula @OGDrac
@gettinfiggywitit So, there's really nothing else to do at night?

Dracula @OGDrac
At least the internet never sleeps. Though, some of you I could do without.

Dracula @OGDrac
I don't have any ulterior motives. I'm just here to brain dump like the rest of you.

Dracula @OGDrac
Since I'm here with little else to do, I thought I'd tell you about my life.

Dracula @OGDrac
Born in Transylvania. Dracul's son, 1431.

Dracula @OGDrac
There were mountains. Dad was important. There was always war.

Dracula @OGDrac
Learned some science and philosophy and art. Extra cultured.

Dracula @OGDrac
Was also imprisoned and tortured. We don't speak of it now.

Dracula @OGDrac
Father was ousted by warlords. They killed him in the swamps.

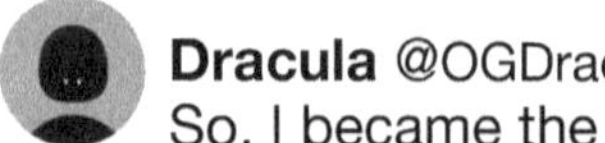

Dracula @OGDrac
So, I became the ruthless killer you all remember. At first, I was fighting back. For retribution. But, then I liked it. My reign of blood.

Dracula @OGDrac
No, not the "I want to suck your" kind. Standard massacre stuff. I was still a living creature then, at least physically.

Dracula @OGDrac
Eventually I beheaded my enemy, Vladislav II. LOL. #victory

Dracula @OGDrac
Back on top. Ruling my beloved Wallachia, except it was in ruins. #sadtime

Dracula @OGDrac
Sooooooo….. I invited the quarrelsome boyars to dinner. Stabbed 'em and impaled them on pikes. #groooossss

Dracula @OGDrac
Liked the impaling. Did it a bunch. Brought order back to Wallachia. #yayme

Dracula @OGDrac
Geez, yes, I realize impaling is bad. But, back then it was in. #sofire

Dracula @OGDrac
They CELEBRATED my reign. Killed over 80k peeps. So, suck it.

Dracula @OGDrac
I don't know why you people have this idea that I'd speak old timey. I've had hundreds of years to change. Duh.

Dracula @OGDrac
Anyway, we were ambushed in 1476 which is where Vlad ends and Drac begins

Dracula @OGDrac
Some of you know about "the Impaler" days. Some of you read Stoker's trash.

Dracula @OGDrac
You missed hundreds of years. I was born anew, killed a LOT more, and then decided to be respectable-like.

Dracula @OGDrac
Ugh… yes, yes, it was well written. A beloved classic. Yadda yadda yadda. It's just not entirely true. #shock #awe

Dracula @OGDrac
Did I know a Jonathan Harker? No. Did I know a similar chap? Yeah, Boggerd Fletchly. You can see why Stokes changed the name.

Dracula @OGDrac
Jonathan Harker, lol. What a name.

Dracula @OGDrac
Anyway, I'll keep this part short. Lots to cover. Lots to cover. It's good there's nothing to do here. You all get story time

Dracula @OGDrac
2500 followers. Picking up speed. #willfollowback

Dracula @OGDrac
Anyway, this lawyer shows up at my lil' castle. I don't remember if there were wolves or not. It's been too long.

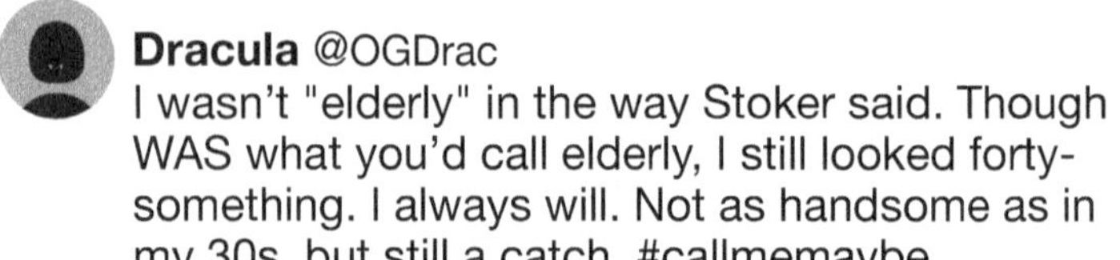

Dracula @OGDrac
I wasn't "elderly" in the way Stoker said. Though I WAS what you'd call elderly, I still looked forty-something. I always will. Not as handsome as in my 30s, but still a catch. #callmemaybe

Dracula @OGDrac
I never kept the lawyer prisoner. The castle was falling apart. There were many ways to leave.

Dracula @OGDrac
Was I supernatural and diabolical? Well, yes. Were there nubile vampire ladies? I wish.

Dracula @OGDrac
I can't speak to the happenings between "Mina" and "Lucy" as I wasn't there. Sorry, folks. #wasntme

Dracula @OGDrac
There seems to be this misconception that I was a ladies' man. Not true. It's been a pretty lonely life. Me and sniveling Reinfeld.

Dracula @OGDrac
@notreinfeld Ugh. You ARE sniveling. Get your deviated septum fixed or something.

Dracula @OGDrac
Yes, Reinfeld and I are still fighting. Let's move on. #personalbusiness

Dracula @OGDrac
Did I feed on "Lucy?" No. Did she have brain fever? Probably.

Dracula @OGDrac
"Lucy" was never undead. At least, not by my hand. Have I fed on people? Before modern meds, sure. #dracbehungry

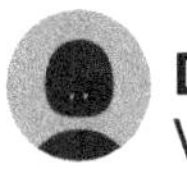

Dracula @OGDrac
VanHelsing blamed me anyway. I hated him. He was very unwoke.

Dracula @OGDrac
So, he pledges to destroy me for something I hadn't done. There were plenty of actual reasons to come after me. His was fictional.

Dracula @OGDrac
This was when crazy old Reinfeld and I met. I've kept him alive all this time because he did me a solid back then. He brought me to "Mina."

Dracula @OGDrac
She was a beautiful mousy creature. I coveted her. As you may guess, the lawyer wasn't keen on this. #sorrynotsorry

Dracula @OGDrac
VanHelsing nabbed her, did some woo woo "cleansing" in my castle and they all tried to destroy me. They didn't. Obviously.But, I left. It was time to move on.

Dracula @OGDrac
Mere moments with "Mina" were still worth it. She was everything.

Dracula @OGDrac
 I don't really know what happened to her. It was hard to keep track back in those darker times. #nointernet

Dracula @OGDrac
Would I have cyber-creeped on her? Yeah, probably. I have my weaknesses. #notperfect

Dracula @OGDrac
Anyway, this was the 1800s. #ancienthistory

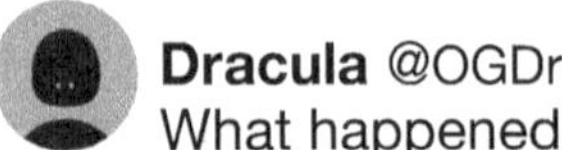

Dracula @OGDrac
What happened next for ole drac? Well, Reinfeld and I traveled. We saw the world, like the entire thing.

Dracula @OGDrac
It's probably why we fight so much. Too much time together.

Dracula @OGDrac
@notreinfeld NOT EVERYTHING IS AN ATTACK ON YOU. Hundreds of years with anyone would be grating.

Dracula @OGDrac
@notreinfeld Yes, even Mina. Low blow, pal.

Dracula @OGDrac
We never stayed anywhere long because I was still killing and eating people. Inadvertently sired a few more undead types. #mybad

Dracula @OGDrac
@gettinfiggywitit I think Bath was my favorite place. I'd kill for a Sally Lunn bun.

Dracula @OGDrac
Not literally kill. I don't do that anymore. Sheesh.

Dracula @OGDrac
There was a cool 40 or 50 years where medical technology advanced enough so I could pinch donated blood to get by, but general technology wasn't good enough to track me. It was a beautiful time.

Dracula @OGDrac
Most people just thought I was some eccentric rich weirdo. They weren't entirely wrong.

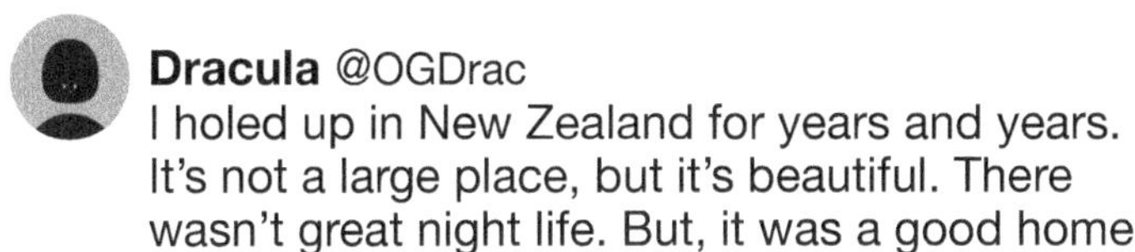

Dracula @OGDrac
I holed up in New Zealand for years and years.
It's not a large place, but it's beautiful. There
wasn't great night life. But, it was a good home.

Dracula @OGDrac
People left me alone. I could enjoy nature, the
great Pacific. No one really questioned my habits.

Dracula @OGDrac
 I did move every 10 years or so because, you
know, I don't age.

Dracula @OGDrac
Sorry this is boring. What did you all think I was
doing? #letmelivemyafterlife

Dracula @OGDrac
Anyway, yeah. So, now I'm here in relative
seclusion spilling my guts on the internet to
people who all think this is a joke, an elaborate
ruse, a publicity stunt.

Dracula @OGDrac
No, I haven't seen Twilight. I don't sparkle. I look
like a pretty normal, albeit pale, man. Occasional
fangage, but not the flippy True Blood kind.

Dracula @OGDrac
They're more like wolverine's bone claws, but in
my mouth. Yes, it hurts.

Dracula @OGDrac
I think Tweeting has grown on me. I don't even
need to say something interesting. No pressure.

Dracula @OGDrac
I wish I could have bran muffins for breakfast.

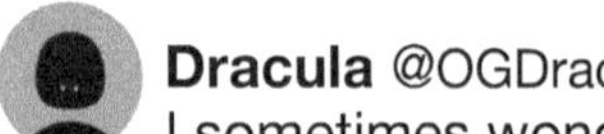

Dracula @OGDrac
I sometimes wonder what'd happen if I were to sink into the Great Lake. Would I be able to walk on the bottom? Could sunlight reach me there?

Dracula @OGDrac
See, I can say whatever's in my head and no one cares. #freeeee

Dracula @OGDrac
I think I should probably catch up on vampire media? What are you reading? Watching? Is it good?

Dracula @OGDrac
Where has Castlevania been all my life? Thank you, Netflix.

Dracula @OGDrac
I probably need to go outside more. The internet is a black hole.

Dracula @OGDrac
But, thanks for the recs, folks. Hotel Transylvania was funny. I definitely don't say "Bleh ble-bleh."

Dracula @OGDrac
I have caught myself saying the occasional "ope" though. #thisplaceisgettingtome

Dracula @OGDrac
Why can't I just be a regular dude? I'm old. I've been bad, but I'm good now. I just want to live my afterlife on my terms.

Dracula @OGDrac
I have explored town a bit more. The nights are growing warmer. The water's flowing again. I think this town needs something more. Something for the night folks.

Dracula @OGDrac
I have an idea. #vaguebooking

Dracula @OGDrac
I think I need some new friends.

Dracula @OGDrac
@notreinfeld No, I'm not replacing you. I'm just expanding.

Dracula @OGDrac
@notreinfeld No, this isn't about a girl. I've literally met no people yet.

Dracula @OGDrac
@notreinfeld Will I turn them? IDK. Maybe, if they want? If I like them? If they're not insufferable like you're being.

Dracula @OGDrac
I think I need a social media break. Someone's getting annoying.

Dracula @OGDrac
@notreinfeld Yes, this time I do mean you.

Dracula @OGDrac
They say it's good to unplug once in a while. Whoever they are… #illuminati

Dracula @OGDrac
Yes, I do like it, but it can't be my whole world. We all need some human/inhuman connection.

Dracula @OGDrac
@notreinfeld It's not like you won't know where to find me. The internet isn't like our only means of communication. I have a cell phone, you know.

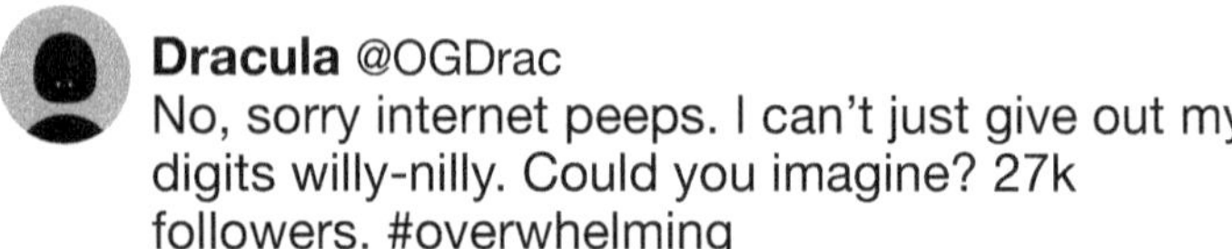

From the journal of Penelope Figgins:

I have always been a night owl. As a young child, I had one of those old-timey portable black and white TV's in my bedroom. The kind of TV that looks sort of like a big clunky old radio, complete with knobs and antenna, the kind your grandfather may have lugged along when ice fishing. I'd be sent up to bed at a normal time, 8 PM, perhaps. But, I could never sleep. Eventually, my mother relented and let me turn on the old television to watch late night shows, usually something David Letterman-adjacent, whatever the old TV would pick up, really.

In the morning, I was dead to the world. I just couldn't get up, didn't want to get up and when someone finally dragged me out of bed, I would be a zombie until well into the afternoon. It was such a hassle that my mother pulled me out of morning kindergarten and I went right into the afternoon class. This sort of thing happens with children, but for me this nocturnal nature never changed. In high school, I'd be up deep into the night watching sitcoms on UPN and falling asleep to *Martin* or *Fresh Prince* around 3 in the morning. I'd crawl out of my cave and stand under the hot water of the shower for an hour, until it ran cold, to try and wake up. It never worked. I'd throw on whatever clothes were nearby and didn't smell, and I'd race to school only to be late, every time. It was lucky that my morning class was usually art. I don't think the teacher ever really learned my name or took proper attendance. So, I made my way through high school with little to no consequence.

In college, I was able to set my own schedule. So, afternoon and evening classes were my preference. Though, there were a few that only ran in the morning. My kind and patient neighbor from across the hall would come and knock on my door over and over and over until I grumbled and said I'd be out. Without him, I don't think I'd have ever gone to or passed my required Political Science course. I'd often just wear my pajamas out the door and certainly looked half deranged in class. But, again, these things aren't out of the question for someone just learning to be an adult, learning to come into their own.

They always told me that the workforce would change me, that I'd eventually get on everyone else's schedule. I believed that. I really did. But, it never happened. We're ten years into my career, one that requires somewhat regular early mornings, and I can wake up if needed, but I'm still up deep into the night no matter what. And, it's not that I have a sleep problem. I don't. I can stay asleep, and when left to my own devices will sleep a normal seven, eight, or nine hours at a time. I just feel so much more alive at night. In my thirties now, I think that all of those peppy morning people were liars and I think they're all a little crazy. I can't imagine a pleasant morning. They're just not for me.

Now, this poses issues from time to time. The whole wide world operates on a different clock. Businesses open and close early, and I am too rural for there to be a wide selection of 24/7 establishments. Even if I was a little closer to the city, those options would be limited to things like diners, casinos, and big bright box stores. While those things are all fine and well, they don't necessarily provide you with the ability to explore or to have a thriving social life (at least one that doesn't make you extremely broke and send you home smelling like your great aunt's ashtray). The world simply doesn't cater to us nocturnal folks.

This is where things get interesting. Just this last year, I began to see local ads for a new attraction, The Night Museum. They were vague though designed with a sort of gothic old-world charm. I wasn't sure exactly what to expect. Would it be a museum dedicated to night time? A museum open during the night? Why are they putting it out in the farm lands and not in the nearby Chicago or Milwaukee? As a girl of the night, I was naturally intrigued. The fact that it seemed slightly macabre was even more of a draw. And, not so secretly, I'd always wanted something like a night museum, a place to go and wander and look and learn, but at night when I felt most alive.

The build up to the opening of The Night Museum was agonizing. I'd become preoccupied by the mystery and intrigue surrounding the whole thing. No one else seemed to share my enthusiasm for the upcoming attraction, instead complaining that it wasn't child friendly or that it seemed like a cheap tourist trap for dummies. Maybe it would be, but I was willing to take the gamble in order to check it out. Finally, the day came. That day, as it turned out, was also my last day.

Approaching the stone facade, filled with an excited trepidation, Penelope gingerly crossed the road in order to get in line in front of The Night Museum. It was 10PM on opening day. The Night Museum was a curious thing. No one knew quite what it was, but Penelope knew it was where she wanted to be.

Finally, she thought. The Night Museum was fulfilling a hole Penelope had always had, a desire she'd never had sated in all of her time on this earth. The museum's hours of operations were 10PM-3AM, each night. Penelope was hoping the place would be something she could frequent often instead of a one-time dud. As she got to the pristine black doors, she was struck by how silent it was. There was noise from a bar down the road, but nothing here, not even on opening night. There was no actual line. No nothing. She couldn't seriously be the only person here on opening night. Could she?

Fingers delicately wrapped around the door handle, she tugged, and that seal gave way to a quiet and dimly lit entryway. The decor was Victorian-esque though modernized a bit, little lamps with pull chains sat atop the front desk and behind it was a slight, though handsome middle-aged man.

Looking up, Penelope was aghast to see a great portrait of a raven-haired young woman with haunting saucer eyes who looked, remarkably, almost exactly like her. "Mina," it read. After having stared, a little caught off guard, for a few moments, Penelope was startled when the proprietor spoke up.

"Welcome," he said, gesturing for her to come up to the desk, "Welcome to The Night Museum." His eyes were wide as he took in Penelope's appearance, darting briefly to the framed painting and back again. "Who are you," he asked in a whisper.

"Penelope Figgins"

A light flickered in the man's eyes, some sense of recognition. "@gettinfiggywitit?"

"Yes, that's me," she replied, still reeling.

"It's me. @OGDrac."

She paused, but only for a second, *Dracula, at last*. This was where Penelope was meant to be.

Dracula moved to the door to lock it for the evening, with Penelope inside. She shivered, but not with fear. The man didn't scare her. He excited her.

Together they explored the museum, trinkets and collections of night-related folklore. Star displays and charts and lights. It was a beautiful love letter to night history. Enchanted by Dracula's extensive knowledge and humorous aire, she listened intently, feeling a kinship to the man, the monster. It was something deeper than lust, though he was charming. It felt like her whole life had led her here.

Dracula, too, felt drawn to this new woman who was so like the one he'd loved long ago. It was as if his Mina had been transported through time and walked right through his museum door. This may have been the best idea, The Night Museum.

"I have crossed oceans and lakes of time to be with you," he mumbled.

"I know," she said, and with a wink Penelope had sealed her fate.

Upon waking, Penelope did leave the museum; she was forever changed, having given herself over to her night nature, the one that had pervaded her life for so long. She would return to the museum each night, to Dracula, partners in proprietorship and in the afterlife.

There were hundreds of years between them, but Dracula felt renewed. Penelope too felt like she'd finally found her way, that this place was home. This feeling was home. Everything everywhere had led them both to this place, this moment, to one another. And, while this is the end of the first chapter, it isn't the end of their story, but instead, a new beginning.

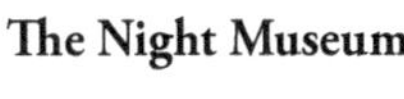

Jessica Gleason is a writer, a reader, a teacher, and an all-around weirdo. She loves horror, fantasy, science-fiction, and sometimes sleeps in a Star Trek uniform. Gleason has been a college English professor since 2008, and is the author of *Sundown on This Town*, *Madison Murphy*, *Wisconsin Weirdo*, and *Damned Before Breakfast*. You can follow her @j.g.writes on Instagram.

Upon the Death of an Adversary

By Jill Protokowicz

The last mourner arrives just after sunset. Dark clouds have stolen what remains of the light sending most of the congregation retreating to more comfortable settings before the incoming storm. Only two diggers remain, and they are trying to fill the grave as quickly as their backs will allow.

When the tall man emerges from the shadow of the cemetery's oldest trees, the gravediggers pause and move a respectful distance. He's American from the looks of the black duster and the ridiculous cowboy hat on top of his head, and yet he glides up the hill with an almost regal quality, his boots barely making a sound over the pile of decaying leaves.

The grave is already half full, so it won't take them long to fill in the rest once he's finished. With an unexpected chance for a break, the older digger pulls out a large flask, one that he had been saving for a job well done, and offers the first sip to his partner.

The mysterious man solemnly removes his hat, revealing a shock of wavy dark hair and pale flesh stretched taut over an aristocratic face. Blue eyes, made brighter by the dark circles under his lids, flicker over to the two diggers before settling back on the grave.

"Man looks like Death's head upon a mop stick," the older digger whispers, taking back the flask of gin from his partner.

The younger man, more interested in what his partner is holding, absently replies, "If 'e falls over, we just push him on in, yah?"

The older man almost lets out a deep chuckle but stops when he feels the cold eyes of the mourner upon him. He watches as those icy blue orbs darken and the stranger lifts his upper lip revealing two long incisors that seem to grow until they rest dagger-like along his bottom lip. The taste of the gin sours in the digger's mouth, and he taps his younger partner on the shoulder, gesturing towards the church.

Dracula watches the two men leave, the elder being far wiser than his apprentice. Once he is assured of privacy, he finally speaks. "Hello, Abraham," he says, looking back down at the tombstone. The passing of Van Helsing's wife three years prior had caused a ready-made memorial waiting for the doctor's inevitable demise. Imagine, coming here to visit his spouse only to be reminded of his own impending mortality. The rest of the site is set up with a smattering of wreaths and flowers, and he wonders if any were from the Harkers, whom he did not see leaving this afternoon's internment.

Behind him, the wind whips through the trees, sending an empty clatter as thin branches clack against each other.

Dracula looks up at the incoming storm, directing the next part towards the heavens. "It didn't take long for death to find its way to your door, did it, old man?" He pauses, as though listening to the breeze before craning his head back down to the open grave. "Of course, you weren't the first. Oh no, poor Doctor Seward, if I recall, found his occupation to be a bit much for him. Weak heart, wasn't it?"

The wind drops for a second, and there is only silence in the empty yard.

"But you, my friend. I honestly must say I thought you would live forever. The way you chased me through Europe made me believe you may be more than just a mortal man." A soft sigh escapes Dracula's lips, and he smiles nostalgically down at the grave. "We had a merry dance together, didn't we?"

The sky begins to open; small droplets of water descend towards the earth. Now, it is Dracula's turn to pause as he allows a moment for nature to mourn alongside him.

Kneeling onto the still dry earth, he brushes away the bit of dirt that had already fallen onto the tombstone until the name Van Helsing is once again pristine. He then proceeds to pull out a carnation from the interior pocket of his double-breasted jacket. The flower was one of those rare hybrids, white with each petal outlined in maroon streaks. He looks down at the changing pattern while rolling the stem absently between his fingers before placing it at the base of the tombstone. "I hope you like it. I got it from a flower girl I ran into on my way here. I may visit her again before I depart."

Sparing a glance towards the church, Dracula checks that the gravediggers are nowhere to be seen before pulling out his trophy: a human heart grasped lightly in his hand. Tacky blood sticks to his fingertips as he brings it to his face for a single lascivious lick. The crimson liquid had already congealed, but fear still clings to its coppery remnants. "And this," he growls, "I plucked from the chest of our old acquaintance Arthur Holmwood. He never did remarry. Such a pity, he had excellent taste in women." Red eyes study the heart once more before tossing it into the grave. Whether the diggers find it or not, makes no difference to him. He will be gone by the time they leave the church.

The rain starts to fall harder, and Dracula stands as the saturated ground begins stain his pants. Bits of grave dirt cling to his hat, and he brushes them off before fixing it atop his head. He looks down at the grave, hearing the soft plink of drops on the brim, before giving a toothy grin. "Do you like it?" he asks his imaginary companion. "It does complete the whole 'American' ensemble, doesn't it? Gives me a bit of an exotic air." Two fingers run along the hat's edge in a mockery of its former owner. "It was Quincey's, I believe. I found it after I crawled out of the charnel pit you threw me in. Took years, Abraham, to pull myself together, but I'm nothing if not patient.

"But you, old man," he spat, "you couldn't hold onto this mortal string for three more days."

He suddenly lunges at the grave, stopping just short of throwing himself in and tearing open the fragile coffin that houses the mortal remains of his greatest adversary. Inhuman teeth gnash in a mouth too small to contain them, and saliva mixes with rain as it runs down his chin. "And now you're gone, and I have no one, no one, but children who dare carry on our feud in your name."

"Tell me, Abraham, did you warn them about me? Do the Harkers know of my return?" Tampering the animalistic desire to feed and destroy, Dracula straightens again as he regains his composure. "No worry, I'm sure I'll find out soon enough." He pauses and pulls out an envelope from his pocket. Pristine white parchment flows back and forth between his hands. "One of my servants intercepted this. You were trying to warn them, weren't you? Jonathan and his lovely wife."

The vampire pauses, running a tongue over his teeth as he tastes her name. "Mina."

Rain is starting to dot the envelope, and Dracula pulls it closer to his person. The only droplets he wants to see touch that white exterior are the crimson color of arterial spray. "Don't worry, I'll deliver your missives when I'm finished draining both of their children and tearing out her husband's throat. Do you think she'll scream, Abraham? Or do you think she'll welcome me with open arms the way she did all those years ago?"

A slight rumble in the clouds, and Dracula stops, looking first to the sky and then back down to the grave as though awaiting some sort of metaphysical retribution. He smiles. "Oh, if only, my friend. I would look forward to seeing you conquer death for one last bout with me."

Crushing the letter slightly, Dracula waits, although he is not sure what he is waiting for exactly. The body beneath him is already decomposing; he can smell the odor of rot and knows that nothing short of a miracle will return this man to him.

Gazing up at the sky, he lets the water drip onto his face in a mockery of tears, or perhaps a salve to make up for the fact that he, himself, cannot cry.

"They say that you died painlessly in your bed," the vampire continues, "but I know that isn't true. Not for us, never for ones such as us."

Another prolonged pause, as he stands preternaturally still in the rain, frozen without breath or life, as though he were a statue that would preside forever over this exalted memorial.

"I suppose what I am trying to say, my friend, is that if I had the power, I would bring you back. I would bring you back so that I could slaughter you myself."

With that, Dracula turns from the burial of his greatest foe and begins his descent to rejoin the world of the living.

He stops at the base of the hill, looking back once more at the half-filled grave, a feeling of joint aching grief swirling through him. Van Helsing had come the closest to besting him, and now here he stands without a true challenger. He looks down at the note and decides to gently tear open the seal in hopes that seeing the words of his rival will give him some comfort.

The parchment inside contains Van Helsing's eloquent script, and he stops when he sees his own name addressed at the top of the paper. His eyes scan the rest of the short letter, crinkling with joy, and he laughs. Perhaps the game is not over.

He lets the paper fall to the ground, water and mud already soaking through the ink, blotting out an old hunter's final words — "Worry not, my friend, I've prepared them for you."

Jill Protokowicz is a struggling storyteller from the little-known state of Delaware. When she's not trying to strengthen her craft, she is molding the minds and imaginations of high school students as a teacher of Literature and Creative Writing.

A devout lover of all things dark and gothic, Jill cut her teeth on the works of Stephen King and Edgar Allen Poe, and their influence continues to resonate in her writing. She became one of the first Creative Writing students at the University of Delaware and furthered her education with a Masters from Rutgers University.

When taking a break from writing and grading essays, Jill can be found chasing after her hyper toddler and equally hyper puppy or enjoying a work of cinematic genius at the local theater.

Dracula:
For One Night Only

By John Kiste

Renfield once told me that Count Dracula was far more personable than he had been portrayed by Bram Stoker. The Irish writer, who in reality had produced his novel based on tales told to him in Dr. Seward's sanitarium by Renfield himself, had captured the master vampire's ability to be charming and showed that trait in the early pages of the novel, but the nobleman had devolved to a stock villain before arriving at Carfax Abbey. Nor had Stoker given any examples of the Un-dead gentleman's hearty sense of humor. Further, Bram also elaborated on Kukri and Bowie knives and the decapitation of Dracula at story's end, but this oversight bothered the famous vampire not a whit.

The sense of humor omission, however, pissed off the Count no end, and though he often sneered at his minion in the belief that the flyeater's tales had been poorly related, he mostly blamed the now long-dead author. And the ridiculous movie versions. As an aside, I feel it should be included, though the Count flatly denied any responsibility for his biographer's demise, the root cause of the Irishman's passing has been laid ultimately to syphilis, which can be transmitted through the mixing of blood as well as by the better-known channels. The infamous vampire was a blood-mixer extraordinaire, besides being an inveterate liar. Food for thought.

Count Dracula once opined, "I have no problem being depicted as a soulless, heartless, bloodsucking fiend. I *am* a vampire. But this nonsense about being humorless—" Then he actually added, "Pshaw!" I had never heard anyone use the expression before; I had to look up the spelling. He flashed his canine teeth in disgust, and I could see them get a bit longer. The whole issue galled him to an addictive degree. Which made sense, since nearly all vampire legends allude to the creatures as incredibly obsessive-compulsive.

"What about that 'children of the night' shit?" he went on. "The 'I never drink—wine' line? You have to time that pause perfectly. I'm not sure Abraham even included it—do you have a copy? How about my forgotten quote to Mina Harker: 'First, a little refreshment to reward my exertions.' I admit it is not Chaplin funny, but it's damn hilarious for a 15th-century Transylvanian warrior. Forgive me, I do go on."

And he did go on. I had approached the Count with the proposal to write a factual bio of his present unlife, but we had reached the point that all he ever spoke of were the glaring exclusions of the earlier novel. He would pace like a caged animal about the ruined moorland chapel where he kept one of his primary coffins, and often he would pause to tear the side from an old pew or rip loose a section of the ancient altar rail. He enjoyed the sudden dramatic sweep of his muscular arm as it created destruction, and he loved watching me cower in my chair. Admittedly, I *was* afraid of him. He was capricious and horribly strong with no possible understanding of morality, but seeing him wreck his own dismal quarters was actually laughable. The fixtures and pews had become so brittle with time that I could have inflicted similar damage upon them.

I had met Renfield first. That crumpled man still existed because, in the end, contrary to Stoker's version, Dracula had turned him. The little minion had such an advanced case of Stockholm syndrome that he posed no threat to his master even as a vampire. He still subsisted on bugs and small animals after more than a century of being Undead, and he shared the graves of suicides during daylight hours, as he had no coffin of his own.

The Count rarely availed himself of the insectivore's services these days, but knew he would loyally attend if summoned. Renfield had read several of my historical works, and had relayed my name to Dracula because he knew of his master's need to set the record straight.

I had been assured of immunity from blood drainage if I agreed to update the *diary*. He also promised not to turn me. I did not desire eternal life. My Franklin Planner runs out in August. The problem was that the Count no longer did anything interesting. I assume he still preyed upon victims in the dark of the city and surrounding towns and villages, but I was not permitted to join him on his midnight rambles, and the newspaper and television reports were oddly devoid of deaths by exsanguination. I made bold to ask how he so cleverly and so completely disposed of his victims, but he merely smiled and showed a lot of teeth. A very original vampire movie I once saw had its bloodsuckers generally make do with bribes at local blood banks, so I satisfied myself with that solution. After all, I knew the Count had gold and cash buried in two dozen places across the heath— he did admit to that.

One chilly night not long before the dawn when I would be ushered out, Dracula hit upon an idea that made his dead black eyes sparkle. "My characteristics are known by the whole world: the clothes, the slicked-back hair, the mannerisms, the fangs. You knew I was the real thing when Renfield introduced us…" I nodded. "I shall book a club. Let folks get to know the real me. It will not even matter if some believe I am a fake vampire, the routine will still resonate, particularly after they have had a few drinks."

I frowned. "Are you talking about stand-up comedy?"

"Why not?" he replied, grinning.

The grin faded when I rejoined, "I think that is a very bad idea, Count." I saw those same black eyes flash red when he thought I was mocking his plan. I recovered at once. "As you said, the audience would recognize you. Some might make it a point to follow you back here come morning." Our moor, our heath, was really just a corner of the Mojave Desert, and there were trails and roads all through it.

"I see," he said, and the fire in his pupils faded. "Not a problem. I can always flutter home."

I knew better than to speak again, and took my leave. Our next session was three nights later, and I found him prancing in a newly dry-cleaned cape. "I've done it," he chuckled, utterly pleased with himself. "I hired an agent, tossed about some coins, scribbled some lines, and booked a 'gig', as you say."

To myself, I said, "Holy Mary on ice skates!" To him, I said, "I'll be there."

And there I was, front row of tables at Tony Jocko's on High Street, eight o'clock Saturday night. The Count was opening for some new talent out of Detroit, and he had splashed around enough unburied monetary sop that he was performing act unseen. I alone knew what he was capable of if he got heckled or jeered, and I had surreptitiously pushed a crucifix into one pocket and a vial of holy water into the other. The sweat ran off me as from an iced tea on hell's front porch.

I had been told more than once that Jocko's boasted mob ties; all I knew was that *someone* made a mint running this dive. The stage and dance floor had not been refinished since Prohibition, and the food and drinks offered little of interest, but every night the city's elite decked out in their finest attire and jockeyed for seats near the band or the entertainment. Tonight I recognized a famous pop singer, a renowned architect, an MLB catcher, a Hollywood screenwriter, and two city councilmen. I also glimpsed Renfield at the bar, but I didn't acknowledge him. The show had the makings of an abattoir.

Suddenly the lights dimmed, the crowd quieted, and the band played Tony Jocko himself onto the stage. The jovial, beefy restauranteur had outgrown his three-piece pinstripe suit, but he smiled as though he had no care in the world—including obesity—as he yanked the microphone from its stand.

"Good evening, ladies and gentlemen—and Stan!" He waved toward one of the councilmen, who guffawed uproariously. "As you know, tonight's headliner here at Tony Jocko's is the latest sensation out of our dingy neighbor to the east, the Motor City: Pete Josten!" The sudden applause bruised my eardrums. "But first, we have a very special one-night-only treat—I think." Jocko winked at the audience. "Ladies and gentlemen, direct from Transylvania, a big hand for the vampire you desire, Count Dracula!"

At that moment insane laughter howled from across the room. I jumped, startled, but knew at once it was Renfield. The other customers were horrified. He had climbed onto the bar, and before security or the bartender could react, he shrieked words similar to ones he had used before. "A red mist spread over the stage, coming on like a flame of fire—" and he held both hands out before him, "—and then he parted it!" Everyone's heads spun back toward the stage, which had indeed filled with a scarlet fog. As they stared, astonished, Dracula stepped through it, dressed to the nines, cape pressed and shoes gleaming. Not a hair was out of place, and no one in the club breathed.

Then, sounding precisely like Bela Lugosi in tone and pacing, he whispered, "Good eev-ning!" The patrons cheered. Well, clever entrance, I had to give him that. I touched the vial in my pocket nonetheless. He smiled wickedly down at me for an instant and turned his eyes to the others. One fine blonde two tables from me had been transfixed by his appearance. He gazed lewdly at her plunging décolletage and licked his lips. "Nice neck," he said. People actually laughed. I downed my bourbon.

Then he began in earnest. "I just flew in from Vegas but my arms aren't tired—'cause I can turn into a bat." These people were drunk, clearly, but most giggled. I felt for the crucifix and said a prayer of thanks. Perhaps we could all survive the evening. He went on. "I burnt my mouth backstage. I think some priest blessed my Perrier. I never drink—Evian!" Yes, it was pure corn, but the Count's eyes glowed and his teeth glittered, and no one knew what to make of him, so they laughed. Some in a stupor of fear, and others because they truly thought he was funny.

"I was engaged to a girl until she put a garlic press on our wedding registry. Some friends said they were spending the weekend at the cape. I told them I wore mine *all* week. They used to say Professor Van Helsing was my mirror image, but I couldn't tell. Think about it." One sloppy drunk was holding his sides in glee and sliding from his chair, and even folks not laughing at the

Count were laughing *at* him. It was strangely contagious. I started to think Dracula had cast some sort of spell. "My agent keeps trying to increase his fee. I told him I hate people who cross me." Pause for chuckling groans. "My dentist is a ruddy fellow, full of blood. When he cleans my teeth my fangs grow—then he charges me extra." Pause for just groans.

He flashed his eyes again, and no one looked away. Except me. I briefly turned to watch Renfield, reseated with his arms crossed, smiling smugly. The Count was back to his spiel. "Tony Jocko was worried I couldn't perform. He said he heard I had a phlegmy coughin', filled with mucus. I said, 'no, it's a wooden coffin, filled with soil." The drunk did now fall to the floor, and sheer gaiety abounded. I saw Tony in the wings slapping his knee in pure happiness. "Truth be told, I've been around a long time. Since the 15th Century. I knew Keith Richards when he was a baby. It's harder to rejuvenate these days. Blood is my Grecian Formula hair coloring. You know the ABO blood group system. A is for ash blonde hair, B is when I want to be a brunette, O is onyx," he ran his hand through his jet black hair to screams of laughter and oohs from the ladies, "like now. AB negative gives one that white streak through everything. Like my friend the Bride of Frankenstein."

The audience roared, and I relaxed in my chair. The Count waved, said, "Fangs! Fangs a lot!" and trotted offstage to thunderous cheering. Tony leapt up and grabbed the mic, shouting, "Let's bring him back out here one more time." More applause. After a minute, the Count stepped back onto the stage. This time his mouth and chin was covered in blood. He wiped at it with his sleeve as everyone quieted.

"Sorry, folks," he grinned, still with the phony accent, though Renfield and I knew the blood was real. "My agent came to the conclusion that I was a real vampire and that he must destroy me." An expectant pause hung thick in the smoky air. The Count suddenly smiled from ear to ear. "That was his first and last missed stake!" The crowd screamed in delight and Dracula bowed and exited. I saw Renfield dashing for the wings. I decided

I didn't know either of them tonight and slunk quickly out the emergency exit.

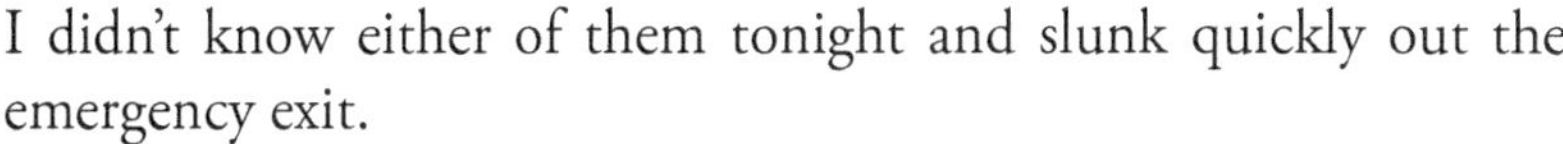

John Kiste is a horror writer who was previously the president of the Stark County Convention & Visitors' Bureau and a board member of the Massillon Museum. He is a double-lung transplantee and organ donation ambassador, a McKinley Museum planetarian and an Edgar Allan Poe impersonator who has been published in Flame Tree Press's Terrifying Ghosts, Third Flatiron, Madhouse Books, Dark Recesses Press, Hiraeth Books, A Shadow of Autumn, and dozens of other anthologies, magazines, and e-zines. He recently won The Dark Sire Award for Best Fiction. You can find him at johnkiste.wordpress.com.

The Historical Dracula

By Sam Ruddick

One night I came home from work and the Historical Dracula was sitting on my couch. He had long hair, a long mustache, very full lips. A long nose. He was not some horror movie caricature with fangs and a cape. He was Vlad Tepes—Vlad the Impaler, the Historical Dracula—sitting on my couch, petting my cat. I recognized him immediately. I knew a lot about him, compared to most people: the purgings of Wallachian boyars, the burnings of the poor and the lame, and, of course, the impalings. Such was his compulsion to impale that, when imprisoned by Turks, he impaled the mice in his cell. I wasn't immediately comfortable with him petting my cat.

I'm not sure I'm comfortable with you petting my cat, I said.

He snapped his head back, hurt and offended. You invited me here, he said. Do you think I would repay your hospitality by doing harm to your cat?

The truth was that I did not remember inviting him anywhere, but when I told him as much he only shrugged, as if there could be no other explanation for his presence in my living room. To be fair, I thought, I might have forgotten. It wasn't as though I had been on the ball in the preceding weeks. I had not been on the ball. I'd been teaching at a community college where they'd decided to offer midnight classes, and I'd agreed to teach a few of them, just to see what it was like. I had done this against the wishes of my wife. She was pregnant and did not like the idea of me being away from the house so late at night. I thought we needed the money. That was my argument. We needed the money because of the baby, I said. But that was only *part* of the reason I'd taken the job. In fact, that was not the reason at all. That was the *ostensible* reason. The *real* reason was that my wife was constipated. It was difficult for her to shit with a baby squeezed against her colon, and being unable to shit made her cranky and sad and unpleasant to be around, and I did not want to be in bed beside her. So I took the classes, not for the money, but to get away from her, and even though she did not *know* this, she *sensed* it, or sensed, at least, that I did not mind being away from her, even when she wanted me most. There was contention between us on the subject of midnight classes. And once there was contention about *one* thing I was doing, I did not mind doing *other* things, in secret, that would have caused contention as well, because she was asleep when I got home from work, and I could smoke and drink as much as I liked. She did not approve of smoking and drinking. I liked to smoke and drink. And don't let the *Hollywood* Dracula fool you. The *Historical* Dracula is more than happy to drink wine. He drank so much wine the first night I had to bring an extra bottle home the next, just to make sure we'd have enough. I don't know how I knew that he would be there again, but the Historical Dracula had given me the impression, without saying as much, that, for the foreseeable future, he was going to be there when I got home every night.

He had impeccable manners. He never gave me any reason to *want* him to leave, and yet I wanted desperately for him to leave. Maybe it was my knowledge of his past. He had killed a lot of people. But if I'm to be honest, I have to admit that his dark side was not the problem. His dark side was fascinating. I wanted to talk to him about his dark side. I was intensely curious. I just didn't know how to broach the subject. What was it like, impaling all those people? I wanted to ask. What is it about *impaling* people that so appeals?

But there was no graceful way to broach the subject. And, as I said before, his manners were impeccable. It elevated you. Put you on your best behavior. You never wanted to be ill-mannered around the Historical Dracula. No, his dark side was not the reason I wanted him to leave. If anything, his dark side was the reason that I wanted him to *stay*. But I could never engage it—could never really *speak* to him about it—because it would have been inappropriate, and the result was that it was intensely awkward being around him. It was like trying to have a tea party with an elephant in the room, only we were drinking wine, and the elephant was a pile of dead bodies you could stack to the moon. I didn't mind him petting the cat. I got to the point, by the fifth or sixth night, where I liked to watch him pet the cat. Because he would never have hurt the cat. So the cat wasn't the problem, either. The problem was that he wanted to watch *Project Runway*.

I liked *Project Runway*, too, but I did not want to watch it with the Historical Dracula. My wife and I were watching Season 9 together, and it would have hurt her terribly had I skipped ahead. It was the only show we watched together. Sometimes, it felt like the only thread between us. The only thing we had in common, apart from the doom growing inside her, pinching her colon shut, so she could not shit or be nice. Being nice is hard when there is a person growing inside you. It's a nice thing to do, a *generous* thing, to grow a person inside you, so I tried very hard to be sympathetic. But I didn't want to hear about her problems with feces. I didn't want to hear about her *colon*. I wanted her to be the woman I'd fucked, not the woman who was pregnant. They were different women. You can't blame them. But you can't drink with them, either. I drank with Dracula. But I did not watch *Project Runway* with him.

What do you think is going on here? I asked. I watch *Project Runway* with my *wife*.

But your wife is asleep, he said, and stroked his mustache. It was an elegant mustache. I usually think mustaches look stupid, but his was so big. It went all the way to his ears, and I wondered what it felt like. If it was soft. I wondered about his mustache, but I did not watch *Project Runway* with him. *Project Runway*, I said, was out. We watched *Law & Order* instead. There was a marathon running on one of the networks. Detectives talking to prostitutes in liquor stores. The Historical Dracula suggested we get prostitutes. I told him I was momentarily light. I didn't have the funds for a decent escort, I said, and I didn't want a ten-dollar blowjob from a woman off the streets.

Besides, I said. I'm a married man.

Dracula said that he understood, of course. He said, I understand why your marriage would pose a problem. I understand about *Project Runway*. She will see that you've skipped ahead, because there will be fewer blue dots on the screen. And even if you could keep her from observing the absence of dots, you could hardly pretend to be surprised when Heidi Klum announces the winner of an episode you've already seen. You could hardly be persuasive, pretending that when you are watching it together, you are watching it for the first time. But the prostitute thing, he said. That I do not understand. Your wife is sleeping. She is constipated. She will never know.

The Historical Dracula wasn't arguing from principle. Principle didn't factor into his thinking about prostitutes. Prostitutes are wonderful, he said, and he offered to pay, and he was so well-mannered, it seemed rude to decline. So I said okay. I got my laptop out of my bag and did a search for local escorts. But the Historical Dracula was already off the couch, putting on his cape, which was not black, incidentally, but thick and red.

I know a place, he said. It's just up the street.

I found it difficult to believe that there was a brothel up the street from my apartment, but he assured me it was there, so we went out into the night and walked up the street, and, as we walked, the street changed. The *architecture* changed. We went from the colonial houses and brick apartment buildings of Boston to an architecture much older, and grander, as though we were walking down the streets of 19th Century Paris. And indeed we were. In a moment, we were in the foyer of a fin de siècle brothel. The madame came out to greet us. She looked shockingly like the Dean of Humanities at the community college where I'd been teaching midnight classes. She had the same thin lips and grey hair, the same rotund torso atop the same surprisingly long legs. But she was much better humored. She seemed to float into the foyer, smiling brightly, as though genuinely happy to see us.

Vlad, she said. How *delightful* to see you.

They took each other's hands, kissed each other on the cheek, and then, still holding hands with the Historical Dracula, the madame turned to me. You brought a friend, she said, her smile more warm than bright now, as though the Historical Dracula had brought her a present. As though I'd been caviar.

Come back to the drawing room, she said. Meet the girls.

She took us back through a velvet green curtain and a set of French doors and then we were in the drawing room, a room without windows that was beautiful just the same, lush and care-free, and in that sense both substantial and insubstantial, its emerald wallpaper, its white couches embroidered with elaborate patterns of gold. There were young women lounging, drinking wine, smoking cigarettes. One of them, a pale, pretty, petite Japanese girl with a stylish bob, immediately stood when we entered the room. The Historical Dracula opened his arms and said her name, *Mitsuko*, and she went directly to his side. He enfolded her in his cape, and they went upstairs.

I was nervous. Embarrassed. Shy. And yet I was immediately drawn to a tall, pale woman on a pincushion settee. All of the women were pale. Dracula had drained them of blood. But this woman was porcelain white and rail thin—emaciated, in fact—with long, lithe arms and sharp elbows, and when she tapped the ashes from her cigarette or lifted her glass to her lips, it seemed as though the parts of her body moved independently, as though she were a marionette, unblinking, controlled by strings.

The madame stood beside me. Who is *that?* I asked.

That's Marionette, the madame said.

I stood in the drawing room door speechless, and the madame touched my arm. Would you like to meet her? she asked.

It seemed impossible that I could meet such a woman, that I could go to bed with such a woman on the Historical Dracula's dime. She had not looked at me when I'd arrived, had not spoken to me, had not smiled like the other prostitutes had smiled, had not beckoned like they had beckoned. But nonetheless, I saw only her, as though everyone else were somehow peripheral, as though she were a work of art, religious in her significance, and the other women merely lights shining upon her. I worried that I was objectifying her, that worship was a form of objectification, but what I felt for her was reverence. I felt lust and reverence simultaneously, as though sex and worship were one and the same.

I can't be with *her*, I said. She's too good.

Rubbish, the madame said, and called to Marionette. Marionette, she said. Come here. There's someone I want you to meet.

Marionette's head swiveled slowly on her neck, like the head of ventriloquist's doll. She had massive curls. Barley curls. Curls like you see in 19th Century photos of children. They'd come into fashion for adults. They were huge and beautiful, and I wondered if she would let me touch them, if they were soft, like, I imagined, the Historical Dracula's mustache.

She smiled unpersuasively. Stood. She wore white lace, and I wanted to set her free. Of course I wanted to set her free. I wanted to save her. She was a whore, and men who fall in love with whores want to save them. I was a cliché out of Victor Hugo. I imagined she had a heart of gold. That was the cliché. The hooker with the heart of gold. She could be a hooker with a heart of gold, and I could save her, I thought. We could live out the whole romance, just as if it had been written in the gritty fairy tales of Victor Hugo: *Les Mis*, or *Notre Dame de Paris*. Realism, we called it, in midnight literature class. We could go for a walk in the rain, I thought. Marionette could worry about her shoes. *My shoes!* she would say.

But she wasn't wearing shoes in the drawing room. She stood barefoot before me, with white, elegant feet. I knelt to kiss them, then remained on my knees because I was convinced that the woman before me was some kind of goddess, even if she was a whore. She lifted my chin, forced me to meet her eyes. I was afraid of them, afraid of their luscious green. She looked down at me and shook her head, telling me without talking that I was wrong. That worship would not be allowed. I got off my knees. She took my hand and led me back to a bedroom, where we made love. I thought we were making love, anyway. I was making love. I *felt* love for her. She did not feel love for me, of course, nor did she pretend to, which made me love her more, but also made me sad, because someone like Marionette would never love me.

She was not, in fact, porcelain. She was a wooden marionette, painted porcelain white. I got splinters in my fingers from touching her, splinters in my cock and my chest, and I asked her if she would be on top and she said no, and I got the sense it was because, if she had been on top, she would have been fucking me, and she did not want to fuck me. She would allow *me* to fuck *her,* but *she* did not want to fuck *me.* She did not want to take an active role in our lovemaking. She was willing to *receive*, to *allow* me inside her, but it had to be clear that her role was *passive.* I wanted her to be active. I wanted her to be on top, to have that view of her body, see the length of her torso and the creases beneath her breasts. I wanted to reach *up* to touch her, to look *up* to see her face, smiling down upon me as she moved on my cock, like a woman who wanted me, a woman in love. She was not that woman. She made it absolutely clear that she was not that woman.

Is Marionette your real name? I asked, and she shook her head, not because the answer was no, but because she would not answer.

It's not going to be like that, she said. I am not that woman.

I respected her for this, even as it broke my heart, because she was so beautiful, and beauty would never love me. I made love to her in the missionary position. I was tender and gentle. I was afraid. I reached my crisis quickly, then lay beside her in silence. She lit a cigarette, and the Historical Dracula arrived. He'd come in like the Hollywood Dracula, like fog creeping under the door, rising into a pillar of smoke by the bed before solidifying into the Historical Dracula. He looked down at Marionette. He said, It's time.

She nodded, tilted her head, and moved a giant barley curl to the side, offered him her throat. He was upon her. She arched her back. She opened her mouth. She trembled. She made a sound like she was coming, a quiet, breathless, tiny cry—a weak, ecstatic gasp—then went limp on the bed. I sat up. I cradled her head in my lap. She was bleeding from her throat. My God, I said. You killed her. She was not actually dead. But she *was* dying. It was clear that she was dying, as clear as it had been that she did not love me.

I asked the Historical Dracula, What is *wrong* with you?

But he only went to the bureau. There was some fresh watermelon on a plate on the bureau. He sliced the watermelon. There is nothing wrong with me, he said.

I looked down at Marionette, used a finger to brush a strand of hair from her eyes. She smiled gratefully, the first authentic smile she'd given me. *Claire*, she said.

I did not understand.

My name, she said. It's *Claire*.

Claire, I said. Oh my God, Claire. I'll call an ambulance.

But she said, No. She said, Let it be. I abandoned my daughter, she said. I left my husband for another man, and my daughter despises me now. She's right to despise me. But she doesn't understand. She thinks I didn't love her. And it was never that I didn't love *her*. It was only that I was confused. I thought I was in love with this man. Victor. I'd known him since we were children, you see? He was my first love, apart from my father. We used to sit on the floor and play with dolls. My father gave me such beautiful dolls. I loved doing their hair, she said, and lifted a hand to her own massive curls. Can you tell?

She smiled faintly, nostalgically, and made a sound almost like laughter.

Victor moved away when we were still children, she said. So I married Joseph. He was the practical choice. A carpenter. The Father of Christ. Hardworking and kind. But a kind man can never make me come. A man's sex isn't *meant* to be kind.

The Historical Dracula laughed from across the room, and I was ashamed, because I had fucked her so tenderly. The Historical Dracula sliced another piece of watermelon while she wept.

Victor made me come, she said. I never meant to see him again. I never hoped or *dreamed* I would see him again. But we found each other on Facebook, and it turned out he was *here*. Right here in Paris!

She shook her head as though the coincidence still amazed her, then dried her face with her wrist, and went on matter-of-factly.

We made plans to meet for lunch, she said. I didn't know I was going to sleep with him. I didn't know that after lunch he would lean in to kiss my cheek and I would turn my head and open my mouth and take his tongue inside me. I didn't know I would take his cock inside me. I didn't know it would feel like I was born for him, like my body was made for his. I would go to his apartment in the afternoons and he would fuck me three times before I had to go back to the Father of Christ, and when we came together it would rain, as though our lovemaking had called the rain down from the sky, and after the rain we would go out to his balcony and smoke and look out over that beautiful treelined street and the wet, trembling leaves, and it was like we'd made the leaves come too. I thought that I could live for Victor. I thought that Victor was my purpose. And when I came home in the evenings my daughter would ask me to sit on the floor and play with her Barbies, but I never did. I never played with Barbies, and I thought that Joseph was better with her, and I was so lonely with him, because he fucked me so *weakly*, she said. He fucked me the way *you* did. As though I were a porcelain doll, rather than a *woman*. It was disgusting. So I left him. I left the Father of Christ, and I left my daughter, because I wanted to be fucked by a *man*. And when I went to Victor and told him what I'd done, he didn't want me. He sent me away, and I had nowhere to go, and now I'm a whore, and I will never enjoy lovemaking again. So please, she said, don't call an ambulance. Because the Historical Dracula has set me free. And as she said this I cried, and my tears fell on her face, and she said, You dear, sweet man. You could never hope to understand. And she died.

I lifted her head from my lap, laid it gently on the pillow and stood, snarling at the Historical Dracula, murdering him with my eyes. I should have known, I said.

The Historical Dracula was puzzled. Known what? he asked.

That being around the likes of you would lead to grief.

Dracula scoffed. The likes of me? he asked. What does that mean?

You murdered thousands of people, I said. You impaled them on wooden stakes and left them to rot, writhing in the sweltering heat and the freezing cold. You immolated the poor and the lame. You're a monster.

The Historical Dracula was visibly offended. A monster? he asked. *Me?* I maintained *order*. Do you think you could maintain order in 15th Century Wallachia *without* the use of horrific violence? He shook his head. He said, Be my guest. I can take you there. Do not think I cannot take you to 15th Century Wallachia. I've taken you to fin de siècle *Paris*. I've shown you *worlds* of pleasure, and all you can show me is sadness. Not gratitude, but sadness. Because a wooden puppet can't love you back. Because you can't be happy loving *her*. She must love you back. Well, if fin de siècle Paris doesn't make you happy, I can take you to Wallachia. We can see how you do. I will give you my throne, he said. But I will *not* let you judge me. You cannot judge me, and you cannot judge Claire. Claire is an *adult*. She knows what she wants. She knows who she is, and she *welcomed* death, so you cannot judge her, and you cannot judge me.

He brought another slice of watermelon to his lips. The juice made his mustache glisten, and—ever the aristocrat—he wiped his mouth. I marveled. How did you do that? I asked. How did you make it sound like her *murder* was a gift?

She wanted to die, he said.

I was enraged. People get depressed, I shouted. After the story she told, it's no wonder she was depressed. And depressed people are suicidal. It's part of the *disease*, you prick. Not an excuse to *kill* her.

But Dracula said, Humbug, and a moment later Mitsuko arrived, and it did not seem appropriate to continue the conversation. Mitsuko was a nice girl. She did not need to hear about women impaled on spikes, or women who would live and die for Victor. She asked the Historical Dracula if he was finished with her for the night, and he said, No, not yet.

So I went home. I left the brothel, walked through the Paris streets until they became the Boston streets, and when I got back to my apartment, the whole place stank of shit—that sweet, over-sweet, sickly smell—the shit of a woman who's been eating Oreos wrapped in provolone cheese, trying to feed the insistent life growing inside her. My wife sat on the couch, petting the cat. I felt comfortable watching her pet the cat. Her smile was sincere. She smiled like an angel and I put my head in her lap and she said, I feel *so* much better, and I said, it *smells* like you feel better, and she laughed, and we watched *Project Runway* together, and now sometimes when I'm driving home at night, I am sorry that I agreed to teach these midnight classes, that our schedules no longer coincide, because I want to be with her again. I want her and only her. But I must confess, when I drive over the Bunker Hill bridge at two o'clock in the morning and the night is thick with fog, I think of the Historical Dracula, and I wonder about his mustache. I wonder if he was right: if my problem all along was that I didn't know how to love.

Sam Ruddick is a PEN/O. Henry Prize-winning fiction writer. His work has appeared in dozens of literary magazines, including (most recently) *The Southern Indiana Review* and *The Sun*.

TOOTHPICKINGS

Back to Blacula

People who study vampire fiction, aside from wasting what could be a lovely afternoon outdoors, often look at the current slate of vampires and what those creatures say about the narratives we tell ourselves about the world today: what does *Midnight Mass* or *Salem's Lot* tell us about our relationship to community? What does *The Vampire Diaries* or *Twilight* tell us about embracing otherness? Others, who also could have chosen to call an old friend or cook a nice meal, will instead look back in time to foundational vampire fiction and ask how we got from there to here: how does *Carmilla* get reinterpreted for a more libertine world? What do we still borrow from *Dracula* and what has been disposed of? And what happened to those vampire-nurturing full moons, anyway?

Both approaches are perfectly acceptable, if you're into that kind of thing. But they often overlook a key turning point in vampire fiction that celebrates its semicentennial this year.

1972's *Blacula*, often dismissed when noted at all, put the vampire into a new context twice over: by grounding the vampire in the history of transatlantic slavery with its reverberations into the 20th century, and by successfully placing the Byronic vampire into modern times. In so doing, the film forged new archetypes and new tropes that are accepted as near canon in vampire fiction today.

Yet it must be acknowledged that the main character outshines the film. The film itself was pushing against the stereotypes and constraints of its time but much of it has not aged well. Some of it will make you cringe. The title character, however, has stood well. Think of Blacula as Iggy Pop and *Blacula* as The Stooges.

If I have a mission, it's not to make you love this film. It's to make you love this character, Mamuwalde, commonly called Blacula. I hope that someday, when someone at Buzzfeed is making their listicle of the best vampires, somewhere between Lestat, Carmilla, and the collected vampires of Buffy, there will be a place for Blacula.

A Synopsis Definitely Not Copy-Pasted From Wikipedia

Prince Mamuwalde travels to Europe with his wife Luva in 1780. Once there, Mamuwalde is turned into a vampire by Dracula (Dracula does exist in the Blaculuniverse) while Luva is left to die in a walled-up room. Sealed in a coffin for centuries, Mamuwalde wakes up in modern day Los Angeles — which is to say 1972 Watts LA. He starts biting warm bodies immediately until — in an admittedly forced coincidence — he meets Tina, who looks exactly like… drumroll… the wife he left behind hundreds of years ago. He begins a romantic pursuit of Tina, littered with bodies along the way, as several men try to "save" her and best Mamuwalde. Mamuwalde aka Blacula wipes the floor with the authorities until realizing that his beloved Tina is dead and that he'll never find happiness. He then walks out into the broad daylight, ending his own life in the sun.

I promise it's better than it sounds.

Is it a gimmick film?

Whether you know the film, or whether you're just a completist and couldn't leave this part of the journal unread, you've probably run across one of *Blacula's* biggest stumbling blocks already. Try this: pause in your read right now and text a non-vampy friend "Hey wanna have a Blacula watch party?" See how many laugh emoji reactions you get. That, right there. *Blacula* gets dismissed by a lot of people, and that title is *not* helping. "Black Dracula" sounds like a gimmick.

And it is! Or it was supposed to be. This film was almost as gimmicky as its title suggests.

So let's take a moment to talk about how this film got made, because that is an important part of this story. It was produced by American International Pictures, a film company so white that their best-known films before *Blacula* were the *Beach Blanket Bingo* movies.

American International — seeing the success of other blaxploitation films — set out to capitalize on its own skill at making cheap horror films, but aim those talents at Black audiences. They generated a screenplay called *Count Brown's In Town* (or *Count Brown Is In Town,* the anecdotal sources vary). Count Brown, by all accounts, was the stereotype of a 1970s pimp with the sparkly cape and cane and platform boots strutting around L.A. biting girls in skimpy clothing. If you are, like me, dying to get a hold of that script, get in line. It seems to have vanished like a cloud of vampire mist.

Why didn't that film get made? Why isn't *Count Brown* the first black vampire on screen? There are two reasons, and they are both named William. First was William Crain — a young, inexperienced, but headstrong director brought on to helm. And then there was William Marshall, the Shakespearean actor with Defcon 2 levels of gravitas. These two both pushed, sometimes individually and sometimes together, to radically change the script. One of the most important things they wanted was for the characters to have, in their words, Dignity.

Dignifying the Vampire

> "After having read them, I thought they really were such garbage, that I knew that I had to do something, if I could, to raise the quality of it."
>
> -William Marshall, *Inside Black Hollywood,* 1975

"I gave the monster dignity in *Blacula* because I needed to get away from the shuffle and jive."

-William Crain, interview with Toothpickings, 2022

How did the Williams accomplish their goal?

First, they surrounded their leading man with a supporting cast that broke from what you'd expect in an exploitation film. The hoes and hustlers were transformed into photographers, pathologists, and funeral directors. Then there was how Mamuwalde presented himself. He was not a pimp stereotype. Not a gangster. He was not any kind of stereotype to be found in exploitation films; instead he was regal, aloof, and oozed nobility. He did have a cape — but instead of loud colors and rhinestones it was black and silver.

Second, the Williams asked writers Joan Torres and Raymond Koenig to add scenes that would place their vampire in a larger cultural context.

The example most often cited as being a defining moment for *Blacula* was its opening scene, where Prince Mamuwalde and Luva appeal to Count Dracula for help stopping the transatlantic slave trade. Tying vampirism into the transatlantic slave trade was the film's opening salvo in contextualizing a story about a Black vampire into something more than a gimmick.

And it makes So Much Sense — are not vampires the ultimate exploiters? It's perfectly logical that Prince Mamuwalde would stop the ultimate in human exploitation by going to the ultimate exploiter of humans — the big daddy of vampires and the reason the journal you are now reading even exists — Dracula. For his part, of course, Dracula has no interest ending the exploitation of human bodies. Instead, he takes Mamuwalde's lifeblood and turns him into a vampire, robbing him of his humanity. Dracula even retitles Mamuwalde — "I curse you with my name" — so he takes away Mamuwalde's name as well. And the result is that Mamuwalde/Blacula is eventually shipped — unwillingly — across the Atlantic to the United States where he's literally purchased in an estate sale like a piece of property.

We all see the metaphor, right? No need to linger on this any longer?

(Aside: there is a debate to be had over how much influence either William had on the writing of scenes like the opening. William Marshall suggested in interviews that he pushed for the opening scene; William Crain insisted that he was scouting locations for the opening scene before Marshall was even cast. Both acknowledge that they didn't actually write the scene, and it must be allowed for that the writers, permitted/instructed to make a better picture that *Count Brown*, came up with many of *Blacula's* best scenes on their own. Unfortunately we do not have the writer's accounts to balance the history.)

In the traditional vampire story, when a vampire is pursuing a human female, the tale portrays the vampire as the outside threat that must be resisted by the woman and the surrounding human males, who form a gang to thwart the othered threat. These are the stories so familiar that we know them even if we haven't read them: In *Dracula*, Mina must be protected from the vampire. In *Carmilla*, Laura must be saved from the vampire. Every virgin in Europe must be kept safe from Varney and Lord Ruthven. This is the familiar, can't-miss vampire plot.

Blacula gave us the vampire's perspective. We get to see his wooing, his courting, his yearning for Tina. Perhaps most important: Tina gets to make the final decision on whether to be the vampire's lover. She is not mesmerized, she is not kidnapped, she is not drained and turned into a thrall. Mamuwalde asks her to come with him and be his lover — while remaining a human — and if she declines he promises to leave her alone. If the promises of Seward and Morris to be Lucy's friend should she reject them as lovers are gentlemanly, what are we to call Mamuwalde's promise?

By 1970s movie standards — which at times let some fairly assaulty things slide by as being romantic — Mamuwalde/Blacula's pursuit of Tina is chivalry incarnate. Even by the standards of the 2020s it holds up pretty well. By vampire standards? It's downright angelic.

For a moment, let us skip over the middle of the film to deal with how it ends (the middle can't be ignored — but it can be postponed a few paragraphs).

If You Want To Kill A Monster, Hire A Monster

Blacula concludes with a suicide, the first of its kind on film. No vampire had ever walked out into the sun willingly prior to *Blacula*. A number have occurred since — *Daybreakers* and *30 Days Of Night* and *True Blood* and *Midnight Mass* come to mind without so much as a Google. Anne Rice had Lestat attempt suicide by sunlight in *Tale Of The Body Thief*. But these are all in *Blacula's* wake. In fact, there was only one vampire suicide prior *Blacula*, in the penny dreadful *Varney The Vampire* published some 125 years before Mamuwalde said "I've had enough of this s%&t!" and greeted Sol's rays.

Professor Jeffrey Weinstock argued in his paper "Vampire Suicide" that such self-inflicted deaths reaffirm the anthropocentric — in other words, living humans and the human condition of mortality are affirmed as a good thing, and that immortality and bloodlust is bad. As humans, we might be a little biased, but let's run with that.

Because it must be said in bold type — **Mamuwalde-as-Blacula hates his condition**. The traditional vampire relishes being a vampire; they revel in their power. Not Blacula! He's miserable in his current form. That's not uncommon now — Anne Rice really nailed this condition and inspired a host of others to explore forlorn vampires, but *Blacula* kicked open the door. There had been a few examples of self-loathing vampires before — *Dracula's Daughter* being a notable one — but with *Blacula* we can begin to draw a line to the remorseful, self-loathing vampires of today, which of course sets the stage for the nice-guy vampires popularized by YA fiction.

Plot wise, what we have here is a monster seeing his only chance for redemption vanish. He chooses to do the one thing that neither time nor God nor the LAPD can do — destroy the vampire. Walking into the sun is a form of surrender for Ma-

muwalde, while at the same time securing a victory over his opponents as he's doing the one thing they've been completely inca-
pable of doing.

Jeffrey Weinstock made another observation in his paper, one
Blacula fulfills:

"(Vampire suicide) functions as an alibi, allowing (the audience) to 'have their cake and eat it, too' — that is, to take pleasure in and even identify with the monstrous creatures that prey
on human life while disavowing them in the end… We enjoy the
bloody mayhem, and then the sun rises, the penitent monster
turns to ash and order is restored."

This gets us into one of the most important things Blacula
brought to the table.

In all the most successful vampire films in the past several
decades, who has been the central character? Has it been the
vampire? It used to be that the hero was the vampire's victim or
vampire hunter, and the vampire was an Other — a distant an-
tagonist. These days, it's rare that the vampire isn't the main character. Guess where that all starts? At least in the movies?

Mamuwalde-as-Blacula is our earliest vampire anti-hero, centered in the film as a villainous, but sympathetic character. We
can't go so far as to say that Mamuwalde is the first sympathetic
vampire — that began almost as soon as vampires started being
big sellers to the public — but he's the first that's the main character, at least in cinema.

Anne Rice really revolutionized the genre with her sympathetic, protagonist vampires, but her books came out after Blacula. One can certainly point to Barnabas Collins in *Dark Shadows*
before this who is sympathetic, but he came on partway through
the series and only developed as a sympathetic character later in
the show's run. *Blacula* knew what it was from the start and
brought it to the movie going audience.

This might be the single most important aspect of Blacula,
that it centered the vampire — the character who, like Black men
in movies, had traditionally been the "other". Let's not lie to ourselves — he's still a villain. He wasn't a bloodless, vegan vampire

who sparkled in the sun. He murdered people. He drank blood. But he had pathos dripping from his pointy teeth.

Why did that happen? In a cheap horror film made in the 1970s, why not just have a monster killing people and be happy with those thrills? I submit to you that, even though *Blacula* was a crossover hit, its first audience was still the same as the blaxploitation audience it was intended for when it was still *Count Brown* — young Black audiences in American cities. And while it was serving up a monster in a Black body, it was also serving up something else.

Watts Are You Talking About?

The bulk of the film is set in Watts. In 1972, that meant something. And while dissecting the unrest of 1965 isn't in the purview of this paper or its author, what that unrest meant for *Blacula* is key to understanding the film.

Suffice it to say, the Watts Riots were big, impactful, and left a lasting impression on the entire nation. And it had not been forgotten seven years later. A simple search of newspapers.com will result in thousands of entries discussing the Watts Riots in 1971-1972, which is understandable given that court cases related to the riots were still being settled at the time of *Blacula's* release.

How the public perceived the riots is also important. Survey after poll after study found that the residents of Watts, and the Black community as a whole, held one group up as being the instigators of the riots: the LAPD. Headlines in 1965 like "Police Brutality: State of Mind?" and "Watts Negroes Blame Job Lack, Mistrust of Police" were common, not just in LA and Fresno where those specific headlines appeared. Whether outsiders agreed or not is immaterial — American International Pictures knew who its audience was and what their opinions were.

In that light, anyone could guess what a royal African vampire does once he gets to Watts. Among other things, he beats the shit out of cops. Regardless of whether he's cornered, outnumbered, or surprised, Mamuwalde always wins the fight. As it turns out, the only character in the film with enough agency to kill Mamuwalde is — of course — Mamuwalde.

Perhaps this is why the marketing advertised Blacula as "deadlier than Dracula": Mamuwalde-as-Blacula is 20-0 against the world, whereas Dracula goes down in the playoffs.

How much time does Mamuwalde spend helping the Black community? Aside from the opening scene in Dracula's castle, zero. But he does let a marginalized community engage in wish fulfillment every time he throws a cop into a wall.

This is what Dr. Robin Means Coleman was talking about in the book *Horror Noire* when she said that, by using the vampire, Blacula was transforming a monster into an agent of Black power. "Blacula," she wrote, "was the decade's gold standard for recreating a White horror classic in the image of Blackness."

The racial dynamics at work in *Blacula* are rarely verbalized. There are only a couple times where anyone overtly says anything about race in the film ("Strange how so many sloppy police jobs involve black victims," mutters Gordon Thomas in one of the few moments of racially conscious dialogue). That's because it doesn't need to be verbalized — it's in the settings, the actions, and the casting. After all, *Blacula* was not meant to be a film that teaches white people about the horrors of racism — the target audience for *Blacula* was already well aware. All the writers and director William Crain needed to do was make the choices that would show the traditional vampire in a new light, and the rest would follow.

Firsties

Before turning to the delights of "firsts": the killjoy stuff:

If you search for "First Black vampire" or "First Black horror film", you will almost always get "Blacula" as the result. That's not totally accurate. The first Black vampire in fiction — and the only one known to exist before *Blacula*, was in the novella *Black Vampyre* from 1819, a book director William Crain, along with most people, had never heard of at the time of filming *Blacula* (in fact, the novella only came to Crain's attention after he and I discussed whether it possibly had any influence on his film. "Do you think there's a prequel for *Blacula* floating around in that story?" he asked). As far as anyone knew in 1972, they were creating the first Black vampire.

There's also a conversation to be had as to whether it was the first Black horror film, since there was a movie from 1940 called *Son of Ingagi* that had an all-Black cast and a Black screenwriter, though a white director. *A Son Of Satan*, an Oscar Micheaux silent film from 1924, might also qualify for the title. Unfortunately, like so many silent films, it is lost.

Regardless, all is well because even if Blacula doesn't get to call dibs on those First Black Vampire or First Black Horror Film, it has an impressive resume, one that still lingers in horror films today.

- First Black vampire *on screen*
- First Black vampire hunter
- First time a male vampire bites another male on screen
- First interracial vampire bite (white-black and later black-white)
- First horror film with a Black director (with a nod to the possibility that Oscar Micheaux *might* be ahead)
- First gay characters in a vampire film and first interracial same-sex couple in any film
- First vampire suicide on screen
- First doppelganger love interest in a vampire movie
- First Hollywood premiere hosted by a Black organization
- First vampire face-changing from "normal" to "monstrous"
- First softening of the vampire from totally villainous to an anti-hero
- First Blaxploitation horror film

But Is It Really Blaxploitation?

Here's a controversy you didn't even know existed — is *Blacula* blaxploitation? Casual commenters will often categorize it that way, but critics and academics are split. A lot of them won't put Blacula into that category.

There is no doubt that Blacula came about to capitalize on the success of blaxploitation as a genre, and it certainly inspired a slate of later blaxploitation horror films, kicking off an entire subgenre. But was it, itself, part of that genre?

What exactly was blaxploitation? Who better to explain than a middle-aged white guy!

Briefly — most observers will agree that blaxploitation cinema encompasses roughly 60 films made in the late 60s and early 70s aimed at a Black, primarily male, audience, centering a Black hero or heroine and surrounding them with a mostly Black cast. Often but not always directed and produced by a white creative team. The films tended to be very cheaply made, and made fast. The stereotypical blaxploitation film had a tough, very macho, very patriarchal leading man (Pam Grier films notably challenged the macho approach, but that's the template her films were challenging).

Why were these films called exploitative? There are a couple theories on that, but the simplest is that the films were exploiting stereotypes of the Black community, in order to make money off the Black community.

Blaxploitation films were popular with audiences — they basically saved a film industry that was in a real downturn after the rise of television and hadn't yet figured out the blockbuster.

But the genre split critics across the spectrum. Huey Newton of the Black Panthers loved it. The Nation of Islam hated it. The conservative *National Review* seemed to both hate it yet revel in the racial stereotypes. *Jet Magazine* loved it. *Ebony* was fairly negative. *The New York Times* had editorials going both ways on the valuc of blaxploitation cinema.

The NAACP didn't like these films, either. In fact, the term "blaxploitation" was coined by a Hollywood NAACP leader who used the term to indicate how little he thought of these movies.

Blacula meets several of the conditions to be blaxploitation. It was cheap, it was made fast, it has a leading man who is very much reinforcing a patriarchal, male-led society, even as he's challenging other systemic issues around race.

But there's some boxes it doesn't check. For one, characters weren't playing easy stereotypes, nor was the resume for each character a rap sheet — the characters were professionals, scientists, artists, and foreign royalty. The film also avoided casting a sports star, which is rumored to have been the original intent when the film was *Count Brown.*

In his important work on Black cinema *Framing Blackness,* Ed Guerrero devotes a lot of space to discussing both Black monsters and blaxploitation. Here's what he has to say about *Blacula* in relation to blaxploitation: Nothing at all. Guerrero's book doesn't mention *Blacula* even once in a long discussion on blaxploitation.

For his part, director William Crain denies that *Blacula* should be categorized as blaxploitation: "I definitely reject blaxploitation to describe any movie that I've done," he stated in a 2022 interview.

No doubt, a booming blaxploitation market made it possible for *Blacula* to get made. American International Pictures wouldn't have dared to make it without the blaxploitation movement. And little doubt that if made as intended when it was *Count Brown's In Town*, it would have fit the bill. But does *Blacula*, in its final form, qualify as blaxploitation? It probably depends on whether you have positive or negative feelings about the genre and whether you have positive or negative feelings toward this film. Love blaxploitation and love Blacula? It's blaxploitation. Hate blaxploitation and hate Blacula? It's still blaxploitation. But love one yet hate the other? Then you'll likely come to a different conclusion.

Okay, But Is It Gothic?

Blacula crossed genres into horror, which had not been done by any other blaxploitation film to that point (if we do indeed regard it as blaxploitation) But it's significant not only that it was horror, but that it was gothic horror. Gothic had traditionally been the playground of white people with money, yet *Blacula* boldly stepped into that space.

Naming *Blacula* a gothic horror is not exactly a hot take; few critics offer an opinion one way or the other on the film's gothic cred, so we aren't dealing with a big controversy here. But if you get interested in vampire fiction, you automatically must start thinking about what makes a gothic story. And while it might not seem it at first bite, *Blacula* qualifies. And not *just* because it's a vampire film.

We have a damsel in distress. We have a Byronic villain. We have a gothic double in Luva/Tina and in Mamuwalde/Blacula. We have oozing sexual tension. We have most scenes take place at night. We have women corrupted by a Stranger.

These are the small boxes Blacula checks. But let's stop to examine a big one.

One leading indicator of a gothic tale is a suspicion of and romanticizing of the Past. And the keywords in that Past? Superstition, aristocracy, sexual terror, and a foreign other from a vague "East". In gothic, modern anxieties are dealt with by projecting onto some far off other — the past, the foreign, the unfamiliar upper social classes.

Does *Blacula* do that? Damn right it does. And it cleverly couches its heroes and villains in such a way that you could be on one side or the other of several class, race, or schools of thought and find a different dividing line for yourself. This essay hits on black and white pretty hard but there have been interesting critiques on how *Blacula* highlights a divide between African American centrism and Afrocentrism, and the suspicions each movement might have toward each other.

In his paper, "Theorizing Historicity, or the many meanings of *Blacula*," Leerom Medovoi declared, "Blacula takes the historical field of meanings associated with the gothic iconography of light and darkness — present and past — and brings it to bear upon African-American history... The vampire Blacula, a master of the 'black arts', becomes a dangerous masculine Other from the gothic past who threatens the modern African-American male self... Blacula is a prince who embodies the imagined virility of ancient Africa for the African-American present."

That's a lot of words to say this: If *Blacula* represents slavery and its aftermath — and remember the films opens with Mamuwalde negotiating for an end to the slave trade and then fast forwards to Watts in 1972 — with a Byronic vampire who's an aristocrat from the vague "East," who threatens the dominion of present day men over their women — which he absolutely does in the context of this film — then *Blacula* crushes the gothic checklist.

And it doesn't matter if you see this film as dealing with black-white race relations, Black American-African relations, or gender relations. It does so in a gothic container.

Blacu-What??

Talk about "dominion over their women" ought to elicit some squirms. I didn't like writing it any more than you liked reading it. But it brings us to the issues in this film, of which there are many. However much I'm an acolyte for the character of Blacula, the movie *Blacula* has a lot to answer for.

First, it doesn't treat women particularly well. Women are either helpless and to be conquered or saved, or they are mouthy and must be put in their place. Tina isn't completely without agency, but she doesn't seem to be the author of her own story.

If the film is less than kind to women, it's downright nasty to gay men. Both the dialogue and the performances are played for laughs and derision. One could make a valiant effort to reinterpret the two male interior designers who are in-love-and-operating-as-equals-while-getting-the-best-of-the-stuffy-old-British-man as Actually A Positive Message. But that's clearly not the intent of the scene.

For his part, William Crain has said that he regrets that treatment in the film. He also told me that he regrets the one and only use of the N-word in the film.

Whether we call *Blacula* a blaxploitation film or not, it's definitely a part of a tradition that was very dick-swinging cis-het-patriarchy reinforcing. *Blacula* may have been challenging some ideas around race, but it wasn't ready to challenge more than that.

Mamuwalde doesn't even seem to soberly grasp the connection between the slavery he tried to end, and modern-day problems he's exacerbating as he goes about turning more humans into vampire slaves. Can anyone break that cycle? If anyone can do it, it must be the supernatural vampire who's immune to bullets, right? But it doesn't seem to be on his agenda.

There are some other weird moments that are less serious. Like the fact that Mamuwalde has been asleep in a coffin for three hundred years, but he knows what a film camera is on the day he wakes up.

Then there's the fact that the whole movie just halts for two and a half minutes while the Hughes Corporation sings, and all the characters just nod and smile. The 70s were great for stuff like that.

And what's with the face changing? It's almost more of a werewolf treatment by way of Jekyll/Hyde — and totally unnecessary. A vampire's superpower isn't fangs or turning into a bat — it's the ability to get up close to a victim without them ever suspecting that you are a supernatural monster. Anyone who sees the blood lusty version of Mamuwalde — awkward fangs, bloodshot eyes, unruly hair, and sideburns that defy logic — would have to run. But the dapper William Marshall in a cape? Pour a drink and lull me with your soothing baritone, dear Prince!

There's the fact that the production value isn't top notch. That opening scene in Dracula's castle? It sounds like it was recorded in a gymnasium with microphones thirty feet from the actors. The most famous shot of the whole film — Ketty Lester running toward the camera in slow motion — goes out of focus.

It's impossible to blame the crew or the talent for these errors — when working with little budget under tremendous time constraints, things like this will get missed. That we still talk about *Blacula* at all today is a testament to how much better the concept was than some moments of the execution.

The Honors?

An area that needs more research — perhaps someone reading this will take it on before I do — is the accolades heaped on *Blacula*. Some of it is anecdotal, some hard to verify.

For example, it's been said that the film single-handedly saved American International Pictures, which was deep in the red before its release. This claim can be found in quotes from people who were a part of the film, including William Crain, and from movie critics. But it has proved impossible for me to verify so far.

Various corners of the internet, including imdb, will point to the Count Dracula Society naming *Blacula* "the most horrifying film of the decade". That's an impressive title in a decade that saw five bigger budget films actually starring a *Dracula*. But this claim is suspicious — AIP had the quote on their marketing materials in the fall of 1972 — a little early to declare anything the best of the decade. Few members of the CDS are still with us, and the only one I was able to contact could not confirm whether the Society ever gave this quote out to *Blacula*.

One honor that can be confirmed is the Academy of Sci-Fi, Fantasy and Horror Films — often called "The Jupiter Awards" — named *Blacula* the Best Horror Film of 1972.

The movie inspired a sequel, albeit with a bigger budget, different director, and completely new cast aside from William Marshall. It also inspired a host of other horror films — an entire subgenre — aimed at Black audiences. More than one contemporary filmmaker has pointed to *Blacula* as paving the way for the modern-day Jordan Peeles of the world.

Final Thoughts

Blacula is an imperfect movie, but it has a leading character who needs to be explored more. The sequel, despite improved production values, disappointed many fans of the original. At this writing, a new Blacula reboot is in preproduction, but it remains to be seen what, if anything, it will take from the original. William Crain is not involved at all and hasn't even been approached.

But I hope that whatever happens, the character of Blacula cedes a place closer to the front of your mind the next time you are thinking about the great vampires in fiction.

Toothpickings, the gothic double of **Brian Forrest**, shapeshifts between written blogs and YouTube videos while metering traffic at the crossroads of vampire folklore, fiction, and pop culture. Toothpickings is currently working on a documentary on *Blacula* director William Crain. To find Toothpickings before the next sunrise, try Twitter or the nearest plot of native soil.

FROM THE GRAVE

Father Pace

By Samuel Marzioli

I was seated in my office, writing notes in preparation for Sunday's Mass, when I heard a tremendous bang against the doorway of the sanctuary. Several eager blows followed, rattling my brain, making tatters of my concentration. I found myself in an outright run to answer it before the mysterious stranger could deliver a third set of nerves-shattering noise.

A man stood outside, leaning on a silver, dragon-headed cane. His skin was pale and his hair black, cut short and kept stiff by gel or spray that made it shine like glass. He wore a black suit with gold pinstripes, and a chain dangled and trailed from his vest's third button into his vest pocket.

"Can I help you?" I asked, taking slow, deep breaths to mask my irritation.

"Not likely," said the man. He smiled, a dull expression absent any cheer, as if the look had been practiced but never truly felt. "May I come in?"

I thought about his request far too long, perhaps, to avoid rudeness. But after a long day of phone calls, meetings, and preparations, I had just one concern: to finish my work so I could get sufficient sleep before the coming Mass. This man, as respectable as he appeared, exuded a certain eccentricity —like a house with a crooked staircase, or a floor with a subtle slant —

that made it hard to believe this would be anything like a short visit.

Offering yet another perfunctory smile, he bypassed my indecision by pushing past me. As he sauntered down the center aisle, he didn't make a sound, not even the leather soles of his shoes as they slapped against the floorboards. I caught up with him when he paused before the altar and looked up at the four-foot crucifix mounted to the wall behind it.

"Is your master in?" he asked.

I laughed, just to be polite. "Yes, always, Mister…?"

"Dracula will suffice."

Once I heard his absurd declaration, I made a face and wondered what sort of motives a man who dressed himself in fine things and legends might have. More so, what he could possibly want with me.

"Dracula? Of course." I smiled, but it soon fell when he threw a dark and stony glare my way.

"Do you think I'm lying? Do you think I'm the sort of man who traipses into churches in the dead of night and cracks light just to please and entertain a priest?"

"No, of course not," I said. "I apologize. I thought you were joking."

"I don't joke, as a rule." He sneered, but the look faded once he spotted the confessionals tucked into the corner of the sanctuary. "Actually, I came for confession, if it's no trouble."

"It's rather late and I —."

"Please. Indulge me."

I nodded, leading the way, stepping first into the confessional booth. He joined me in the adjacent compartment. Darkness choked the interior, but before I could adjust the lighting, I noticed two bright, red spots glowing through the screen separating us — monstrous eyes, or so I was meant to think. I laughed, though I managed to pass it off as a fit of coughing. Whatever he had to say, I prayed it would be quick.

"Bless me father, for I have sinned," he said.

A lengthy pause followed. When this had occurred before, it usually meant one of two things: either the person was hesitant to admit how long it had been since their last confession, or they weren't Catholic and had never learned the ritual correctly. Call it a personal bias but I decided, in regard to this man, it was probably the latter.

"You must realize confession is for Catholics," I said. "Someone who has been baptized, confirmed, and has taken part of the Holy Eucharist."

"Yes. I was hoping you could make an exception."

"That's not how it's done."

"Then make it so," he snapped, his voice reverberating between the sanctuary walls.

I fixed him with a patient look, focusing on the red glow that was meant to be his eyes. "All I meant is that while I am able to give you a friendly ear, I can't offer you absolution."

"As you wish. Shall we begin?"

"Please," I said, shifting in my seat.

"I'm a murderer of men, women and children, and of that I am without remorse."

"A murderous vampire?" I asked.

"Yes, obviously. Does that bother you?"

"As a work of fiction or the trappings of an adopted identity? No, not really. But as a glorification of violence, it most certainly does."

"Fiction? Whatever made you think it's that?"

I pursed my lips. "You may proceed, but be aware that I may withdraw my offer to listen at any time I feel your intentions are not, shall we say, correct."

"Yes, that is your right." He paused. "I'm the son of Vlad Dracul II, a Voivode of Walachia, and Princess Cneajna of Moldavia. Being born into royalty, I came to expect all the wealth and pleasures that a princely life entailed and spent most of my days and nights indulging in my every whim.

"But by my eighteenth birthday, I lost all sense of purpose and meaning. I had a burning in my heart, a longing for something that could transcend the banality of existence. To that end, I sold my soul to the devil."

"You didn't," I said, sarcasm pouring from my lips before I could stop it.

The man eyed me patiently and blinked twice. "Of course, I do not mean that literally. No crimson man with a contract appears when one seeks to make oneself anathema. It's a process, one which I started by taking innocent lives — and I did so with vicious glee. I tortured many to the brink of death, and when they were made to suffer even longer than they had dreamed possible, I took their lives with my bare hands.

"Afterward, I drained their bodies of their essence, their blood. When that no longer proved efficacious, I drank it like a fine wine. At first, I found the flavor salty, metallic, and abhorrent. It made me nauseous, and when I indulged too much, I vomited for hours. But with persistence, one can grow accustomed to anything, and soon it sat and settled in my stomach with ease.

"One day I knew I had finally gone too far. After I'd engorged myself with blood, and even flesh, I stumbled from my palace, half-drunk and in an ecstatic state, and fell to my knees beneath the full force of the sun. Do you know what happened then, priest?"

"Can't say that I do," I said.

"It was during the first moment of my new existence, when my transformation began. In that instant, that brief flicker of time where my old mortality and my rising immortality intersected, I stared up into the sky and saw a face. Bright and penetrating, like a host of stars had gathered to burn as one shining light.

"I gazed into its eyes, almost sacrificing my vision to its endless glory. For those who have never experienced such a thing, I cannot explain it. Suffice to say, I realized then that I wanted its attention, to be the focus of its magnificence, more than anything I had attained through my own corruption. But the moment — no longer than a heartbeat — passed, and the face turned away from me. Though it came without words, the message it conveyed was all too clear: I had been abandoned, once and forever."

"Whose face do you think it was?" I asked.

"Who else? The face of God."

As undignified as it seemed, I had to admit I was beginning to enjoy myself. Confessions were usually a dull affair where someone admitted to taking the Lord's name in vain, or having an impure thought about their secretary, or yelling at their spouse or kids or dog. This, however, was something else. Because of the passion, the conviction, the remarkable details of his story, I drifted to the edge of my seat in anticipation.

"What did you do next?" I asked.

"What could I do? I was like a man who, after finding his wife dead, held a gun to his temple and pulled the trigger — only to see her rise, alive and well, in that split-second before the bullet ripped his life away. There was no going back."

He leaned toward me so that his red eyes almost pressed up against the screen. "And, I suppose, that's why I'm here. I'm tired. My weariness weighs on me like chains of unfathomable proportions. Call it an existential crisis if you wish because I am certain that's exactly what it is. I yearn again for purpose and meaning and can never find it the way I am now."

"Even the simple act of coming here has to mean something, don't you think?"

The man retreated, leaned back against the farthest wall. "Perhaps... A thought does occur to me. True contrition is impossible, but what if an evil performed against evil can create a sort of good? What if I murder my body? Maybe that sacrifice would be enough. And if so, perhaps God will look upon such an act as a necessity through which all my misdeeds can be excused, because of the greater good it will achieve. Does this sound plausible to you, priest?"

I chewed the inside of my cheek. Sham or not, I had heard this kind of sentiment before, right before someone dragged a knife down the center of their wrists, or swallowed an excess of pills, or threw themselves from the top floor of a high rise. The fun had ended; it was time to get serious.

"No, don't talk like that," I said. "Life is a strange, circuitous journey, filled with both tragedies and joys. You can't judge the future by the problems of today. There's a saying I once heard, trite but true: suicide is an eternal answer to a temporary problem."

Silence, so I continued, "I have some phone numbers for people who might be able to help, people who are far more experienced than I am at this sort of thing. Should I get them?"

"This isn't about suicide."

"Then what is it about?"

"Have you heard nothing I've said, or are you a simply a fool?"

"Neither."

"Then you don't believe me?"

I hesitated.

"Ah, there it is." The man chuckled. "I sensed your doubt, of course, but didn't realize its depth. You think I'm mad, rambling on about blood and God and dark bargains."

"What I believe about the truth of your story isn't —."

"You think, maybe, I'm a fraud? That I spend my days avoiding the sunlight to achieve a pasty complexion, with surgically implanted canines, seducing men and teenage girls with equal abandon?"

The way his eyes moved in the darkness of his compartment, I could tell he shook his head. He sighed and then fixed those glowing circles back on me.

"Before, you said your bar-napkin proverb was trite. Please bear in mind that what you are about to see is no less so to me."

His eyes vanished. Smoke poured through the clover leaf pattern of the screen that separated us. It gathered into a single mass inside my compartment and then expanded into a swirling pillar out of which the man solidified, piece by piece. Once the process finished, he loomed over me, staring condemnation.

We studied each other for some time before I collected enough courage to say, "Let's talk outside."

He opened the confessional door and stepped out, and I followed. My mind raced with possibilities. Either this was an elaborate con of amazing quality, or else I was actually face to face with the monster this man claimed to be. How could I be sure?

The old stories spoke of various vampire vulnerabilities, such as their susceptibility to blessed water, and especially crosses. To that end I strolled over to the front of the sanctuary, leaving the man standing just outside the confessional door. I grabbed the rosary beads that I'd left on the ambo, hid it behind my back and returned the way I came.

"What's this feel like?" I said, holding the image of a crucified Christ before his face.

He let out an exasperated sigh, cocking his head as if deciding what to do. He raised his hand. What happened next occurred faster than I could follow. Whereas once his fingernails had been the neatly trimmed and polished pink of a well-manicured hand, they soon transformed into black, jagged claws, like five glistening obsidian knives.

"Oh God," I whispered, breathlessly.

His lip curled into a snarl and those knife-claws drifted to my neck. Right then, I was convinced this was no trick — and he was no man. I believed my life was over and that he'd drain me and leave me as a withered corpse, rotting on the sanctuary floor. I closed my eyes, swallowed hard and prepared myself for the end.

The very next second, I felt him slip away. My eyes shot open and followed him —a blur of motion that only slid into focus when he reached the front door and faltered.

"Wait!"

Even now I don't know why I said it. Perhaps curiosity got the better of me, but I choose to believe it was because I felt true pity for him and his incredible story.

"What is it, priest?" he said, turning to meet my stare.

"Don't go. While listening to you, I did believe you were mad. Look at the times we live in. The things society produces, adopts, and worships leave one unprepared for anything but crackpots and fools. Vampires? They're the stuff of paranormal romance novels and erotic fantasies, not reality. Or so I thought."

He laughed and this time a sliver of true humor warmed the edges. Without even realizing he had moved again, I found him standing in front of me.

"What now?" he asked.

"That's what I was going to say."

"Is there any hope for me?"

"Hope?" I gripped the rosary tightly in one hand. "No, probably not."

"Then what can I do? What is expected of me?"

"I've always believed Scripture to be a survey of divine truths, not an exhaustive, systematic work."

"And?"

"And your kind is left out, never mentioned, not even in passing. But what if we could discover the answer to your particular problem through some more general principle? Wouldn't that be enough?"

"Explain yourself."

"You said before you were willing to take your own life? Saint John once wrote, 'Greater love hath no man than this: that he lay down his life for his friends.' There's truth in that, even here. And though the teachings of the Church strictly forbid suicide for its sanctified members, I can't imagine any other way for you to seek absolution other than to do exactly that."

The vampire scoffed. "You're a little too eager for me to die. It makes me wonder if it's my best interest you're after."

"I fear you, sure, any reasonable man would. But for me it's no more than I would fear anyone that was capable and willing to cause me bodily harm, or death. No, if what you say is true, if you truly believe everything you shared, I will help you in any way I can."

The vampire looked away.

"What do you need?" I pressed.

"Be with me until the end. Pray for me when I die."

"I will."

I sucked a breath and closed my eyes so tight I could see red roiling in the blackness behind my eyelids. Then I let the air out, crossed myself twice and kissed the rosary. Together we sat on a pew in the front row.

The vampire looked forlorn and yet a shade of madness stirred within his eyes. I thought of a wolf caught in the jaws of a leg-hold trap, whimpering from the pain, but no less capable of ripping out the throat of the hunter who had ensnared it. I wondered if, like the wolf, his weakness was temporary and any minute now he'd declare his true intentions and strike me down.

"You're still afraid," he said.

"Does that bother you?"

"No. As they say, what is courage without fear? Are you ready, priest?"

"Yes."

"Then take my hand."

I took his hand with my left and placed my right on top of his. His skin felt cold, hard as granite — exactly as stories had led me to believe. With his free hand, he put his claws against the side of his neck and held them in place. He hesitated, made as if to speak.

"What is it?" I asked.

"It may interest you know that I originally came here to kill you. Once I said my piece and there was nothing left between us but the farce of our meeting, your death was the inevitable conclusion. How it has changed from that to this, I'll never know." He shook his head and closed his eyes. "Goodbye, priest. Perhaps I'll see you again someday, in another place."

With that, he dragged his claws and the skin of his neck opened in four deep, jagged stripes. His head toppled from its perch and thumped against the pew, rolled onto the floor where it finally settled. No blood followed, not a trickle or a gush, which didn't surprise me — not now. When his body turned to ash before my eyes, and his hand disintegrated between mine, I prayed to God that this monster, this once-man, would find the peace he wanted and not the destruction he deserved.

In any case, Dracula was dead. For a moment, I thought about the irony of this figure of legend and horror ending his existence as a vampire slayer. Perhaps it was always meant to end this way, a sort of cosmic punch line to a tragic and gruesome life. Once I considered all this, I spoke the words of absolution slowly, almost in a whisper. I still couldn't decide whether doing so was a waste of time or an absolute necessity. Either way, having done all I could do, I committed him into the hands of God.

Afterward, I got up to fetch the broom and dustpan to clean up the mess that he had left behind. Whether Dracula found what he had been looking for or not, his body was still an unclean thing. And unclean things had no place, even in death, even as ash, on the grounds of a holy temple of God.

A slightly different version **Father Pace** was published in Stupefying Stories issue 1.8, October 2012.

Samuel Marzioli is a Filipino-American writer of mostly dark fiction. His work has appeared in numerous publications and podcasts, including the Best of Apex Magazine, Flame Tree's Asian Ghost Short Stories, and LeVar Burton Reads. His chapbook *Symphony of the Night* was released by Aurelia Leo and his collection *Hollow Skulls and Other Stories* was released by JournalStone Publishing. You can check out his infrequently updated blog at marzioli.blogspot.com.

LAST RITES

The Role of a Lifetime
By Jessica Lévai

I stand before my castle, fresh return'd,
My latest shoot successful, one more film
Completed. Rain drips from my armor, pools
About my feet. Inside, I drop each piece
Of costume to the floor, as once I dropped
More modern clothing, crisp tuxedo suits,
And yards of ebon capes with crimson lined.
My slippers on, I leave the pile behind.

I'm on my own tonight. My lovely brides
Are on another project. I don't care
When others get the spotlight, whether it's
Wry aesthetes from New Orleans, spark'ling boys
A-brood in high school, or quartet of clowns
From Staten Island. Soon enough, my phone
Will ring, and I'll pick up. Nobility
Has obligations. I will leave my home,
Become a monster, lover, warrior,
Or joke. Whatever suits their need. My mind
Recalls that famous actor (What's his name?)
Who asked they drape him in his vampire cloak
When laying him to rest. He lies somewhere
In costume evermore. I sympathize,
I even envy him his sleep, but please,
That fellow was an amateur. Rebirth
Is painful, glorious, and wearying.
It is not always good to be the King.

I trade the rain for shower spray and shed
The long dark locks, the widow's peak. An itch
Starts on my palms and upper lip as hair
Sprouts back. Beneath the blood-warm water all
My chiseled muscles wither. I emerge
A pale and thin old man. My coffin calls.
I snack on rats that scurry past. I lift
The lid and slide inside. The hour grows late.
I check my phone's connection, sigh, and wait.

Jessica Lévai has loved stories and storytellers her whole life. After a double major in history and mathematics, a PhD in Egyptology, and eight years of the adjunct shuffle, she devoted herself to writing full-time. You can find her work at Strange Horizons, Cossmass Infinities, and Tor.com. Her first novella is *The Night Library of Sternendach: A Vampire Opera in Verse*, which won the 2022 Lord Ruthven Award for Fiction. She dreams of one day collaborating on a graphic novel, and meeting Stephen Colbert. Check out her website, JessicaLevai.com, for links and more.

www.ingramcontent.com/pod-product-compliance
Lightning Source LLC
Chambersburg PA
CBHW060500300726

48975CB00008B/2577